KNIGHTHUNTER

ORONIS KNIGHTS
BOOK 2

ANNA HACKETT

Knighthunter

Published by Anna Hackett

Copyright 2023 by Anna Hackett

Cover by Ana Cruz Arts

Edits by Tanya Saari

ISBN (ebook): 978-1-922414-88-5

ISBN (paperback): 978-1-922414-89-2

At Star's End – One of Library Journal's Best E-Original Romances for 2014

The Phoenix Adventures – SFR Galaxy Award Winner for Most Fun New Series and "Why Isn't This a Movie?" Series

Beneath a Trojan Moon – SFR Galaxy Award Winner and RWAus Ella Award Winner

Hell Squad – SFR Galaxy Award for best Post-Apocalypse for Readers who don't like Post-Apocalypse

"Like Indiana Jones meets Star Wars. A treasure hunt with a steamy romance." – SFF Dragon, review of *Among Galactic Ruins*

"Action, danger, aliens, romance – yup, it's another great book from Anna Hackett!" – Book Gannet Reviews, review of *Hell Squad: Marcus*

Sign up for my VIP mailing list and get your *free box set* containing three action-packed romances.

Visit here to get started: www.annahackett.com

CHAPTER ONE

Pulling the hood more securely around her face, Knightmaster Nea Laurier strode down the dirty street.

To one side, the ugly, brown city of Daibos pulsed with noise and energy. To the left, the vast spaceport that the tiny planet of Drov was known for stretched out as far as she could see.

A huge Nillian freighter flew overhead with a low drone. She paused, watching its rusted, over-patched hull slide past.

It was almost always nighttime on Drov. She wrinkled her nose. It was so different compared to her bright, beautiful homeworld of Oron. The Oronis prized art, symmetry, nature, and beauty. The city of Daibos was its antithesis—brown, drab, and dirty. It was known for the spaceport and its corrosive acid-rain showers. The buildings were all made of reinforced metal, etched and stained.

She kept moving, peering through the mesh fence to scan the ships in the port. She was looking for a particular one.

She moved the folds of her robe, looked at the scanner that she held, and studied the data on the screen. The stealth trail of the ship she was hunting had stopped here. The ship had landed at the Daibos spaceport. Her jaw tightened. She *had* to find that ship.

The ship was carrying the abducted Oronis Knightqueen Carys, and her head knightguard, Sten.

Nea would not fail.

She was a knightmaster, like her father before her. He'd taught her duty and honor above all else.

And that failure wasn't an option.

Lumbering ground transports moved past her on the street. Probably carting cargo to and from the port. She scanned her surroundings. There was no one else on the street.

She activated her combat implants and leaped over the port's security fence.

She landed in a crouch on the other side, narrowly avoiding a puddle from an earlier acid-rain shower.

Nea rose, and stared into the shadows as she moved deeper into the spaceport. As a trained knight, she'd been taught to move with stealth. She paused against the brown hull of a small cargo ship. Ahead, she spotted some smaller passenger cruisers parked in an orderly row.

The scanner in her hand vibrated, and she pulled it out. Her heart rate spiked.

The trail was growing stronger.

Yes. Energy zinged through her system. *Please, let the knightqueen be close.*

Suddenly, she heard grunts, followed by guttural voices.

Gul. She swiveled and ducked under the hull of the ship. There was an indentation on the side, around the exhaust ports. She climbed into the space and curled her leg up, letting the shadows mask her presence.

The thud of heavy footsteps sounded. Two aliens came into view.

She gritted her teeth.

Gek'Dragar.

They both had tall, broad humanoid forms, with the addition of long, sturdy tails. Their scaly skin was a pale gray that darkened toward the top of their heads. Two ridges ran along sharp cheekbones, and four bony horns—two on each side—swept back from their faces. One had long, black hair tied back at the base of his neck, while the other's hair was a shade lighter and hacked off at his shoulders. Deep-green eyes glowed in the dim light.

They were the mortal enemies of the Oronis.

Centuries ago, there had been terrible wars between the Oronis and the Gek'Dragar. Many Oronis knights had lost their lives defending their people. They'd beaten the Gek'Dragar, and the aliens had retreated into the depths of their own space.

Until recently.

After irritating incursions along the Oronis border, the Gek'Dragar had launched a brazen attack on the Oronis capital, and abducted the knightqueen.

Nea blew out a slow breath as the Gek'Dragar passed. These two were just port workers, not soldiers.

Oh, but she wanted to attack. Her hand flexed. She'd been trained to fight. The deadly combat implants combined with her relentless training made her an excellent knight.

Her father wouldn't allow anything less.

Knightmaster Torquin Laurier had a reputation for drive and persistence. He'd expected the same from his children. He'd been training her, critiquing her, and quizzing her, from the time she could walk.

And expecting her to always follow the rules, to be the best, and to do everything with honor for the knightqueen and her people.

Nea released another breath. She needed to focus on the mission, and not her impossible-to-please father. She climbed out of her hiding spot and hurried along the side of the ship. The scent of spaceship fuel and the sharp, chemical smell of acid filled her senses.

The Gek'Dragar ship had to be close. And Nea hoped that meant the knightqueen was close as well. She paused, then darted across an open space between some ships.

There was a roar of engines, and a ship lifted off nearby, its landing lights illuminating the ground. She sank back into the shadows.

Once the ship was gone, she continued on. She turned a corner, and found herself face-to-face with a port worker.

This one wasn't Gek'Dragar, but another species, a Phidean.

He had skin with a pink undertone and three horizontal ridges across the bridge of his nose. The side of the ship beside him was open, a toolbox and other parts littered around him where he was working. The male's liquid-dark eyes widened, and he lifted his tool.

Without asking any questions, he attacked.

Nea dodged. She kicked him, and when he staggered, she landed a chop to his arm. He grunted and dropped the tool. It clattered on the concrete.

With a low roar, he snatched up another tool off a nearby crate. This one crackled with energy, glowing a bright blue. He swung it at her.

Gul.

She dodged, but his next swing was fast, and he clipped her arm. Stinging pain hit her, and she clenched her teeth.

She leaped back and tripped over a discarded part. She fell onto the dirty concrete, swallowing a curse.

The Phidean advanced, an ugly smile on his face.

Suddenly, a dark shadow detached itself from a nearby ship.

It attacked the Phidean from behind. The newcomer landed a hard blow to the Phidean's lower back, where the alien had sensitive organs. The Phidean made a strangled sound.

He dropped the electro-tool, and the dark shadow yanked the Phidean backward. Nea heard the distinctive sound of a neck snapping, and watched the port worker's body drop to the ground.

The shadow stepped forward, the light catching his face. Nea hated that her heart gave an annoying thump.

He was tall, all hard-packed, lean muscle, and his short, platinum-blond hair a bright glimmer in the darkness. The sliver of light highlighted his high cheekbones and haughty face. She couldn't make out his ice-blue eyes in the darkness, but she had no trouble picturing them.

"Having a little trouble, Knightmaster Nea?"

Gul, she hated that drawl.

"I had it handled." She rose, dusting off her robes.

One pale eyebrow rose. "It didn't look that way."

She fought back a hot spurt of annoyance. "I can take care of myself, Knighthunter Kaden. I don't need you or anyone else to take care of me. I'm a knightmaster."

A slow smile crossed his face. She hated that it made him more attractive. He'd been striking at the Academy as a teenager, as well. Females had always been panting after him.

He'd been her nemesis. Taunting her, annoying her, playing pranks on her. She hated him, and that overconfident aura of being in charge of everything that he gave off.

No one was in charge of her.

"Don't worry, Nea. I won't tell anyone that I rescued you."

You can't punch him, Nea. She met his gaze.

He smiled. "I can almost hear all the names you're calling me." He reached out a hand.

She tensed.

His fingers brushed over her cheek, and tingles spread over her skin. She sucked in a breath. It must have had to do with the electro-tool that hit her, not him.

"You had a smudge of dirt," he said.

She knocked his hand away. For better or worse—and right now, it was a *worse*—he was her partner on this mission.

"Let's find the ship." She spun and started walking.

She felt a prickle on the back of her neck. A part of her hated turning her back on him.

He was a knighthunter—part spy, part assassin. They couldn't be trusted.

Plus, he was Kaden Galath.

He *definitely* couldn't be trusted.

HE LOVED WATCHING Nea's long-legged stride.

Especially when she was angry.

Knighthunter Kaden Galath followed his partner deeper into the spaceport. One part of his mind took note of the different ships around them, but most of his focus was on Nea.

Drov was near the border of Gek'Dragar space. It was a hub for trade and cargo, and lots of different species visited, lived, and worked here.

It was also a cesspool. Lots of unscrupulous types did business here.

As a knighthunter, it wasn't his first trip to Drov.

He and Nea were keeping their identities under wraps. If the Gek'Dragar guards spotted any Oronis knights... Well, they'd end up with a fight on their hands. Their priority was the knightqueen, and Knightguard Sten.

The queen's guard had managed to get a dura-binding on himself and the queen. The tether couldn't be removed without killing both of them. It had been clever. It meant the Gek'Dragar had been forced to take Sten, too.

Kaden's mouth pressed into a firm line. He hoped they were both still alive and unhurt. Kaden held onto the fact that if the Gek'Dragar had wanted Knightqueen Carys dead, they would've killed her instantly, not abducted her.

Nea suddenly halted, looking at her handheld scanner.

Kaden let his gaze run over her fit body. Even draped in a robe, he could tell from the way she held herself that she was in good shape and could take care of herself. Her black hair was hidden, but the hood just accented the bold lines of her face.

His gut tightened. He'd wanted her from the first day at the Academy.

Beautiful, smart, athletic. She came from a well-respected Oronis family. She always did the right thing, followed the rules, and helped people. The perfect knight.

For a boy who'd come from nothing—worse than nothing—she'd seemed like perfection.

And she would never, ever be for him.

Kaden had worked hard to keep a gulf between them. At first, it was to protect himself. He knew that letting people close put you at risk.

As he got older, it was partly to protect her, as well.

He was constantly drawn to her. Even at the Academy, and far too many nights since, he'd dreamed of Nea —naked, under him, taking him deep, sucking his cock.

He swallowed a curse. They were on a dangerous planet, in enemy space, and the last thing he needed was his hard cock getting in his way.

Kaden drew in a deep breath. He needed to keep Nea safe, and that included from himself. He'd never sully her, or drag her into the darkness with him.

If he had to have her hate him to do that, so be it.

He saw her frown. "Nea?"

"We're close." She turned ninety degrees, and walked between two parked ships.

Voices ahead caught his ear. His implants were attuned to the tiniest sound vibrations. All the enhancements that a knighthunter needed for spying.

He grabbed Nea's arm and spun her. She let out a quiet gasp, but was smart enough not to speak. He pressed her against the side of a ship, his body flush with hers.

As she drew in a breath, he felt her full breasts against his chest.

Gul. He met her gaze. Even cloaked by shadows, he could still see her aqua-blue eyes.

The voices got louder, and she stiffened. They stared at each other, as whoever it was passed by on the other side of the ship.

Once the sound was gone, Nea shoved him.

Kaden didn't move.

"Back up, Knighthunter," she whispered.

"When I'm ready."

"The universe doesn't revolve around you." She shoved him again.

By the coward's bones, she was gorgeous. "It does when we're sneaking around enemy territory."

Her eyes narrowed. "You're a bossy *gul*."

"And you're stubborn." He stepped back. He always liked that about her, except when she ran herself down.

He remembered at the Academy that she liked to ace all her tests. She was so stubborn, and she'd stay up all night studying, and not eat or sleep enough.

She was the same on missions.

Well, he wouldn't allow that on this mission.

She stalked off, then stopped, staring ahead. He followed her gaze and saw the Gek'Dragar cruiser. It wasn't too old, but was nothing flashy.

Nea looked over her shoulder. "That's it."

His gut tightened and he nodded.

They moved together swiftly. He pressed a palm to the panel on the side of the ship and used his implants to link to the ship's computer.

"The security system isn't active."

Nea's face twisted. She knew, as he did, that it meant they were unlikely to find the knightqueen aboard.

Kaden activated the door, and it slid open. A short ramp extended.

They strode inside.

The first thing Kaden saw was the large cell at the back of the ship. It contained two narrow bunks. As Nea went toward the rear, he cleared the front of the ship.

There was no one aboard.

"Kaden?"

He strode toward her. She was crouched in the cell.

She pointed, and he saw the markings scratched into the wall. A straight line with two triangles above it. A sword and crown. The symbol of the knightqueen.

"They were here," he said.

Nea rose, her face grim. "But where are they now?"

CHAPTER TWO

The knightqueen wasn't here.

Nea knew the likelihood had been small, but it was still a punch to the gut.

"We need to access the ship's records and port security footage," Kaden said.

She glanced at him. "Agreed."

"If we can discover where they took her and Sten..."

Never give up. Her father's voice echoed in her head. *Get up, do better.*

She nodded and turned. There was a small control tower with a circular dome on top. The spaceport command center. "We need to get in there."

"It'll be heavily guarded."

She glanced back over her shoulder. "Afraid, Knighthunter?"

He cocked a brow. "I'm more worried that you are."

She headed for the door of the ship. "Hardly."

As she stepped outside, he moved up beside her. His scent hit her. Something dark and spicy. She kept her face blank. It didn't seem fair a man she hated smelled so good.

"Any aftereffects from that electro-tool back there?" he asked.

She snorted. "Like you care."

He sent her a long look.

"I'm *fine*," she said. "It's so sweet you care."

"I don't. I just can't have you passing out in the middle of breaking into the command center."

Asshole. She rolled the Terran word around in her head. The Terrans had become their recent allies.

Nea hadn't been sure about them, at first. Earth was a distant planet, less technologically advanced than Oron. Initial signs had pointed to them aiding the Gek'Dragar to abduct the knightqueen.

As it turned out, the Gek'Dragar had framed the Terrans. Sub-Captain Kennedy Black of Earth had helped, along with the crew of the Terran ship the *Helios*, to find a way to track the stealth trail of the Gek'Dragar ship that had transported the queen.

Kennedy had almost died in the process, and the head of the Knightforce, Knightmaster Ashtin Caydor, had fallen in love with her. Ashtin was the coolest, most controlled knight Nea knew. And now he was in love.

She shook her head. Ashtin was back on Oron with his new love, and Nea was here with the most annoying man in the universe, on a Terran ship in Gek'Dragar space. The *Helios* had been the only ship capable of sneaking into Gek'Dragar space undetected, and tracking the stealth trail.

The unexpected upside was that Nea had learned a

few useful Terran words. Like asshole. It was the perfect description for her current mission partner.

They passed several parked ships as they approached the command center tower. She had to reluctantly admit that he moved well, was fluid, and didn't make a sound. He'd had lots of practice, of course, on all his secretive missions. That was a sour thought. He'd barely practiced at the Academy, and everything had seemed so easy for him. Instead of studying and training, he'd kept busy pulling pranks on her. Once, he'd put an *uvoll* in her bed. A tiny, but ferocious, creature.

Asshole.

Kaden held up a hand. He spoke straight to her implant.

Two guards. Coming this way.

She nodded. They hid in the shadows by some storage crates.

The guards passed by, and Nea noted that they were armed with stun sticks and disruptors. Once they were gone, she and Kaden hurried to the door at the base of the tower. She watched Kaden press a palm to the control panel.

As his gaze turned inward, his implants busy interfacing with the computer, Nea scanned the area around them.

The door beeped. They slipped inside.

"I can't freeze the cameras from here," he said. "I'll have to do it from the command center. Move fast and try to stay out of sight."

She nodded.

He jerked his head, and they jogged up the stairs.

The large room at the top of the tower was circular, with a large bank of computers. Before they could make a plan, she watched Kaden lift his palm. Red energy crackled across it.

He strode in, like some avenging knight of old. There were two bored-looking workers who started in their chairs. Their eyes widened, right before Kaden hit them both with the energy bolts.

Red energy crackled over their bodies, and they fell out of the chairs, shaking.

"We should have made a plan first," she hissed.

"No time." He leaned over the control screen and started swiping. "We need to take care of the security cameras and erase our presence."

She huffed. She was a knightmaster. She was used to planning battles and fights, not sneaking into places.

Nea was direct. She fought with honor and came in through the front. Kaden was the kind of man who snuck silently in through the back.

"Done." He straightened. "I'm hooked directly into their system. Searching now for the record of when that ship landed."

"Why is your energy red?"

His gaze shot to hers. His face was all sharp lines, with high cheekbones, but his mouth was far too sensual.

Stop thinking about his mouth. She kept her gaze steady on his. All Oronis knights had combat implants. Their main implant, the oralite, was a nano implant that grew into a knight's brainstem and powered all their abilities—armor, weapons, enhanced senses.

The energy of the oralite was blue.

For every knight, except this one.

"A genetic mutation," Kaden said, abruptly.

It seemed like a quick, pat answer. She sensed there was more to the story and opened her mouth to ask.

"Found it," he said suddenly. "The ship arrived a day ago."

The screen under his palm flared to life, displaying the security feed of the ship. As they watched, the side door opened. Several Gek'Dragar left the ship, clutching weapons and scanning the area. On alert.

Two more marched down the ramp, escorting their prisoners.

Carys and Sten.

Nea's heart leaped in her chest. The queen was alive. On the screen, Carys looked rumpled, her dress—once grand and beautiful for the ball—torn and dirty. Despite it all, however, her chin was held high. Around one slim wrist was a glowing band that linked her to the man beside her.

Knightguard Sten Carahan was a little older and a lot more seasoned. He was tall, with very broad shoulders, and a body formed of slabs of hard muscle. His brown hair was short, and his features rugged. One cheek was covered in scars he'd gotten protecting the queen from a long-ago attack.

Sten was limping, one eye swollen shut. He'd been beaten.

The Gek'Dragar guards led the pair off the ship, and disappeared deeper into the port.

Were they still on Drov? Nea hoped so. They were *so* close to finding them.

"Here." Kaden switched to different footage. This showed Carys and Sten being led onto another Gek'-Dragar ship. It looked smaller and sleeker. A new design built for speed.

Nea's stomach dropped.

As they watched, the ship lifted off.

"No." She slapped a palm against the console.

"Patience, Knightmaster. We have the ship." He smiled, looking pleased with himself. "And we have its signature. We can track it."

She blew out a breath. "Okay."

"I've saved all the relevant data."

She knew they couldn't risk an off-planet transmission to the *Helios*. It could be detected. They needed to get back to the shuttle they'd used to come down to the surface, then return to the *Helios*.

The sooner they did that, the sooner they could track that Gek'Dragar ship and find the knightqueen.

And the sooner they found the queen, the sooner Nea could be rid of Knighthunter Kaden Galath.

KADEN KEPT pace beside Nea as they strode down the Daibos street.

They had their hoods up again, trying not to attract any attention. Their shuttle was parked on the other side of the spaceport. It was easier for them to circle around the spaceport than pass through the heavily secured parked ships.

They had visual proof that Carys and Sten were

alive. They'd been here. Kaden felt a tightness in his chest. He *would* find them, no matter how long it took.

The knightqueen was loved and revered. She ruled Oron with grace and fairness, but she had a core of steel. She could make the difficult decisions when required. Her parents had been loved as well. The previous knightqueen and her consort had been good rulers, who'd been killed by a Gek'Dragar assassin.

They couldn't lose Carys.

Beside Kaden, Nea appeared to be lost in thought. He knew how dedicated she was. At the Academy, she'd always been top of the class. She liked doing everything right, and being the best.

Unlike him, who was happy to bend the rules to get the job done. He'd learned at a very young age that he had to fight for food, safety, and survival. He resisted the urge to clench his hand into a fist.

Until he'd been taken off the street and put into an Oronis care home, he'd never even had a bed to sleep in. And until he'd befriended a small, dark-haired boy who'd come from nowhere as well, he'd never had a friend.

Those two boys had dreamed of being knights one day, of being someone.

Now Ashtin was a knightmaster, and Kaden was a knighthunter.

Their jobs suited both of them. Ashtin was made to be a leader, and Kaden was made to work in the shadows. He was good at it.

The muffled thump of music and a burst of laughter came from ahead. Some sort of club. It was a pop of color among the dreary gray and brown buildings. Neon lights in pink and blue blinked. There were people standing outside, smoking something with a pungent scent.

He and Nea walked past swiftly, ignoring the calls to come and join in the fun.

"I hope we can track that ship," Nea said.

"We will. We won't stop until we find them."

She met his gaze and nodded. The aqua-blue shade of her eyes always made him think of bright island waters.

All of a sudden, two large shadows stepped out of an alley ahead of them, and blocked their way.

Nea stopped. Kaden glanced behind him. Two more hulking shapes were closing in.

One of their accosters stepped forward, and the weak streetlight highlighted the man's gray, scaled face.

Gek'Dragar. Tension ran down Kaden's spine. Did they know who he and Nea were?

"Give us your valuables," one of the aliens rumbled. His voice was deep with a low rasp.

Nea straightened. "No. We aren't easy prey, you *gul-*lovers. Find someone else to harass."

The leader took another step closer, his tail swishing behind him. "Then give us whatever you downloaded from the spaceport command center."

Gul. These were no simple thugs. Kaden turned, keeping all four in sight.

"We have no idea what you're talking about," Nea said.

"Fine." The lead Gek'Dragar clapped his big hands together. "I'll have to make you tell me."

Groans escaped the Gek'Dragar. Their bodies started

to morph, and grow bigger. Muscles swelled, and their clothes ripped. He saw claws growing on their hands.

The *var*.

By the coward's bones. It was a change the Gek'-Dragar could induce. They got larger, stronger, more beast-like. There were legends about Gek'Dragar warriors rampaging on the battlefield.

Kaden met Nea's gaze. They shared a second of understanding.

They both threw off their cloaks. Nea activated her combat implants. Black bands snapped around her body from the implants along her spine, her armor forming.

Kaden followed suit. He watched her visor slide over her face, a second before his did the same.

"*Oronis,*" one of the Gek'Dragar hissed.

Kaden watched as information on his opponents scrolled across his visor. He threw his arms out, his red energy crackling on his palms and running up his forearms.

Beside him, Nea's blue energy lit up the darkness.

The four Gek'Dragar charged them.

Kaden's blood sang with energy. Fighting was something he'd been born to do. It spoke to the energy that lived inside him.

He shot two energy spikes at the two Gek'Dragar behind them. Nea's energy ball slammed into the lead Gek'Dragar.

But it didn't hold them back for long.

The *var* meant they wouldn't feel pain. With a roar, one of the Gek'Dragar pulled a combat sword off his back.

Nea whirled and landed a kick to one alien's knee. He lurched. She leaped into the air, and her next kick connected with a second Gek'Dragar's head.

The alien shook his head, shaking off the blow. The *var* made the ridges on his face thicker and his horns longer.

Nea's sword formed in her hand—long, and glowing blue. She spun and attacked the incoming Gek'Dragar.

Kaden formed two swords. His favorites were twin curved blades. They were shorter, but in his hands, deadlier.

He whirled, ducked, and dodged. He sliced up his two opponents.

Cut. Slice. Hack.

He whirled again, his blood heating. His blades sliced across scaled skin.

Soon the Gek'Dragar were bleeding from numerous cuts, which was slowing them down. He saw Nea leap and slide her sword into one Gek'Dragar's chest. The alien froze, then dropped with a tortured groan.

She landed, lunged, and took out another one.

She was magnificent. He could watch her all day and night.

Kaden crisscrossed his swords and beheaded another Gek'Dragar.

The final one staggered back. He tried to run, but a blast of Nea's blue energy lifted him off his feet.

"Kaden!"

He spun and his heart jerked. Nea stood, holding an energy bow in her hands, notched with a glowing blue bolt.

She had it aimed right at him.

His mind emptied.

"Down!" she yelled.

He dropped.

The energy bolt sizzled as it passed over his head. He heard a deep grunt.

On one knee, Kaden whirled.

A fifth Gek'Dragar had been sneaking up on him. The bolt had pierced the alien through the chest. He tipped forward and collapsed onto the dirty street.

Kaden rose.

Nea strode toward him, her bow dissolving away. There was a smug look on her face.

"You're welcome," she said. "Now, let's get off this planet."

Kaden watched her and smiled. "For once, Knight-master, we agree on something."

CHAPTER THREE

Nea strode onto the bridge of the *Helios*. She knew that Kaden was right behind her. He didn't make a sound, but she could sense him. A part of her didn't trust him at her back.

The knighthunter sure could fight. The way he'd moved...

She shook her head. She needed to keep her mind off the infuriating man.

She met the gaze of Captain Attaway. The Terran woman was in her mid-forties, and one of the most respected captains in Earth's Space Corps. She had a straight bearing, and blonde-brown hair that she wore in a short, no-nonsense style.

Beside her stood Chief Engineer Watson. The engineer was probably ten years older than the captain, with graying hair she wore in a messy bun, and a weathered face. She had a grizzly temperament. A young, male ensign was with them, his dark-blue Space Corps uniform neat and tidy.

They were part of the skeleton crew of Terrans who had volunteered for this mission. They'd all earned Nea's respect in a short time.

"No luck?" the captain asked.

"The ship landed here. Kaden and I saw a visual feed of the knightqueen and her guard. They were still alive."

Captain Attaway nodded. "That's some good news." She cocked her head. "But I have a feeling there's bad news, as well."

Kaden crossed his arms. "They were moved to another ship that left the planet shortly after they arrived."

"Damn," Chief Watson muttered.

Nea held up a chip she'd already used her implants to manufacture. "We've got the signature of the second ship. It's Gek'Dragar."

The ensign took it and hurried off to a console.

The captain eyed Nea, then Kaden. "Did you encounter any problems dirtside?"

"Nothing we couldn't handle." In Nea's head, a picture formed of red, curved swords, flashing. He'd moved so fast. A deadly whirlwind.

"Okay, I've got it," Ensign Noth called out.

An image flashed on the screen showing a trail moving away from Drov and deeper into Gek'Dragar space.

"They're using the same stealth method of the other ship we tracked," the ensign said.

"Blackwell, follow that trail," the captain ordered. "Maximum speed."

"Yes, Captain," the pilot at the helm replied.

Under her feet, Nea felt the ship's engines rumble to life.

The chief engineer frowned at the screen. "The signature's a little different than what we were following before. I'll need to tweak our equipment to account for that."

"Will that be a problem?" Nea asked.

"No. It shouldn't be."

"Nea, while you were on the planet, we sent an update to Knightmaster Ashtin," the captain said.

Nea straightened. "Is everything all right on Oron?"

"He said the people are concerned for Knightqueen Carys, but Ashtin assured them that the Knightforce are doing everything to bring her home." The captain paused. "There was a communiqué from your father, as well. You can access it on any computer console whenever you want."

Nea's muscles tensed. "Thank you." She turned and saw Kaden watching her.

"I'll be in the gym if I'm needed." He bowed his head. "Knightmaster."

She caught herself watching the way his black trousers clung to his ass and muscular thighs as he strode out.

"Knightmaster?"

She jerked and saw the captain looking at her. The chief engineer was giving her an amused smirk.

"I'll listen to that message now," Nea said. "Thank you."

She moved to a console on the other side of the

bridge. She tapped the controls and a second later, her father's distinguished face appeared.

Torquin Laurier had a wide, strong jaw, gray hair he kept well-cut, and heavy brows that always gave him a thoughtful look.

"Nea, I hope you're progressing with your mission."

"Yes, I'm fine, father," she muttered to herself.

"The knightqueen's recovery is of utmost importance. *Nothing* is more important."

Her heart squeezed. Not even his daughter.

"You must go above and beyond, Nea. If you fail, you'll bring shame to the Laurier name."

She felt that familiar heavy weight sink onto her. She pressed her fingers to her temple where a headache was forming. She looked at her father's imposing, authoritative face. She remembered him smiling, long ago. She had memories of him tossing her up in the air as a child. At least she thought they were real, and not just wishful thinking. It had been before her mother had died. Back then, he'd been softer, more loving.

But after Fiora Laurier had died of a virulent alien fever, her father had turned his focus to his children being the best Oronis knights he could make them.

Then her older brother had died...

Nea felt a pang. She missed Maurin. He'd teased her, always checked in on her. He'd been a good knight and a wonderful brother.

His death had made her father harsher, less forgiving.

On the screen, her father gave one decisive nod. "Good luck, Nea."

The message ended.

That was it. No "I love you" or "be safe." She sighed and shut off the console.

She needed to burn off some steam. Ordinarily, she'd go to the gym, but she didn't want to run into Kaden.

The man saw too much.

The captain had told her about a small, exercise pool with a swim current generator aboard the *Helios*. It was for the captain's own private use, but she never used it, and had offered it to Nea if she ever wanted to use it.

She was going to swim off her frustration with the mission, her father, and with a certain knighthunter.

KADEN WOKE IN AN INSTANT. Asleep one second, then in the next heartbeat, awake.

He was in his cabin on the *Helios*. His implants told him that he'd been asleep for four hours. Then he realized what had woken him.

The engines had stopped.

He sat up and pushed the covers off. He pulled on black trousers and a black shirt, then slipped on his shoes.

He was out the door in three seconds and jogged toward the bridge.

A moment later, he spotted Nea coming down another corridor. She wore loose, gray pants and a blue shirt. She flicked a glance at his chest, and he hid a smile. He knew the compression shirt clung to his physique.

"Do you know what's wrong?" she asked.

He shook his head. The bridge doors opened, and they walked in together.

Captain Attaway stood with her hands clasped behind her back staring at the viewscreen. The woman was in her uniform, but her hair was a little mussed and there was a crease on her cheek from her pillow.

"Captain?" Kaden said.

She glanced over. There was a fierce frown on her face. "Our engines have overheated."

Chief Engineer Watson's face appeared on the viewscreen. She was sweaty and looked pissed. She was down in the engine room.

"Running our stealth camouflage generator constantly is putting extra exertion on the ship's systems," the chief said. "It's partly burned out some of our parts. We're working to fix it."

Nea stepped forward. "Is the stealth mode still activated?"

"For now, but it could die, too, if we don't get the engines fixed."

"We are in Gek'Dragar space, Chief," Kaden said. "If they find us..."

"Yeah, yeah, I'm well aware, Knighthunter. Thanks for pointing out the obvious."

The sarcasm didn't bother him. He liked that the engineer always spoke her mind.

"We're sitting ducks," Captain Attaway said. "It's an Earth saying. We used to hunt ducks...which are a bird..." She waved a hand as her voice trailed off. "But thankfully for now, we're hidden ducks."

There was a low drone and the lights on the bridge flickered.

On the screen, Chief Watson cursed. "Now we're visible sitting ducks. The stealth generator just failed."

Captain Attaway straightened "Chief—"

"I'm on it." The engineer waved a tool. Her skeleton team rushed around hurriedly in the background.

Kaden glanced at the viewscreen. They had no engines, and no stealth. This was *not* good.

"We aren't near any planets," Nea said, her gaze on the viewscreen. "Just a small nebula."

If they got lucky, no one would detect them.

An alarm started beeping.

Captain Attaway cursed. "Ensign?"

"Captain, we have a small group of ships on long-range scanners. They're on the other side of the nebula."

The captain's mouth flattened. "How many?"

Ensign Noth raised his head. "Six. They're small ships, but they're too far out for me to tell what they are, exactly."

"I can tell you," Kaden said. "They're a Gek'Dragar long-range patrol. They fly small, Garga-class patrollers. Pilot and copilot inside." He paused. "They'll be armed."

"Great," Nea muttered.

"How long until intercept?" the captain asked, her jaw clenched.

"They're increasing speed," the ensign replied. "Twenty minutes."

Kaden stared at the glowing dots flying in formation. Yes, a ship seeming to appear out of nowhere on their scanners was something they'd be very interested in. "Knightmaster, how are your flying skills?"

Nea's brow creased. "I beat you at the Academy in our flying classes."

"Barely. I just thought you might be out of practice."

Her eyes sparked. "I am not out of practice. *Ever*."

"Good. Then come with me. Captain, we'll take two of your fighters out and see if we can deal with our incoming friends."

Captain Attaway nodded. "We do have weapon systems online, so we're not totally defenseless."

He nodded and swiveled. As he strode out, Nea fell into step beside him.

"I haven't flown Terran fighters."

"I'll send you the details and schematics now." He used his implant to send the information to her. "The first thing I did when we came aboard was study the Terran fighters. Just in case."

Nea blew out a breath. "If the Gek'Dragar identify us and send a message to their central command, we'll lose any element of surprise. It will put the knightqueen at risk."

"Then we'd better not let them identify us, or get a message out."

They reached the flight bay, and two glass doors opened for them.

There were several small, sleek fighters docked in the hangar.

The fighters were vaguely triangular in design, made from gray metal with touches of blue on the side. They had two large engines at the back, and a clear canopy over the pilot's seat. They also appeared to have decent laser cannons.

"Flight suits are over there." He pointed to a rack on the wall.

He shed his clothes and pulled a fitted suit on without missing a beat. When he lifted his head, Nea quickly glanced away.

"Turn around," she said.

"Shy?"

She glared at him.

"Fine." He spun and listened to the rustle of clothing. He breathed deeply, his mind happily providing him with a vivid image of what Nea looked like naked.

"Let's go," she said.

The dark suit clung to every curve she had. He gritted his teeth, trying to find some control.

As Kaden approached the closest fighter, the clear canopy slid back. He climbed in and checked over the controls.

"They aren't quite as maneuverable as an Oronis fighter, but they are fast," he told her.

Nea climbed up and settled into the fighter beside his. She nodded, her face all concentration as she studied the controls.

"Ready, Knightmaster?" He smiled at her. "Don't worry, I'll have your back the entire time."

Her gaze narrowed.

Gul, he loved her quick temper. She was so easy to rile.

"I'll have *your* back, Knighthunter." Her canopy closed.

Kaden closed his and started his fighter's engines.

"Kaden, docking bay doors opening," the ensign's voice came through the console.

Ahead, the large doors opened, lights flashing around the opening. He touched the controls and his fighter lifted off, the landing gear retracting.

He shot out of the *Helios*.

His body was pressed back into the curved seat. A second later, he saw Nea follow him out of the ship, her fighter soaring up beside his.

Time to take down some Gek'Dragar.

CHAPTER FOUR

I t didn't take long for Nea to get used to the controls of the Terran fighter.

She would've liked to practice on it a bit, but that wasn't an option. They needed to buy the *Helios* some time to get the engines and stealth generator back online.

And they needed to down all six Gek'Dragar ships. They couldn't let them report to anyone.

Kaden drew his ship up alongside hers. She saw his profile through the canopy and briefly wished again that he didn't look so good.

She remembered having the same thought at the Academy when she'd first seen him. He'd been striking, even when he'd been young. His face all interesting angles and his blue eyes like chips of ice. Mostly, he'd ignored her, or given her self-satisfied smirks. Then he'd started to tease her, usually for spending too much time in the Academy library. For always being the teacher's favorite. Even now, she remembered her embarrassment, the heat in her cheeks. Her pain that the boy she thought was gorgeous, didn't like her.

Well, she wasn't a child anymore.

"We're getting closer," he said.

The ships weren't in visual range yet. She saw the nebula, a beautiful mix of colors—teal-green, brilliant blue, bright-pink.

"Visual range in thirty seconds," Kaden said.

Nea kept her gaze straight ahead.

There.

The first Gek'Dragar ship came into view.

It was made of brown metal. They had a half circle shape at the back, with a long semi-circle of glowing engine ports, and the bow narrowed to a point where the weapons sat. The cockpit sat in the center.

"They're increasing speed," she said.

"Because they think they've spotted easy prey."

The Gek'Dragar were hunters at heart. Militaristic. Driven to overrun and rule others. Her jaw tightened.

All six ships were visible now.

"Kaden, alpha seven attack formation?"

His low chuckle came across the line. "I like the way you think, Knightmaster."

His ship shot off to the left.

He liked the way she thought? She shook off his praise, and she flew to the right.

As she raced in closer to the Gek'Dragar, three ships broke off to intercept her. The other three raced toward Kaden.

She threw her focus into the fight. She hadn't had a decent space battle for a very long time.

They came at her in a *V* formation. She smiled and threw the Terran fighter into a sharp dive.

The Gek'Dragar flew overhead. She pulled the ship into a hard turn and whipped around behind the Gek'-Dragar ships.

Kaden was right, the ship wasn't as maneuverable as she'd like.

But it would do.

She opened fire.

Blue laser fire streaked toward the Gek'Dragar. The lead ship of the *V* exploded.

The other two peeled away.

"Oh, no, you don't." She gave chase.

They dipped and turned. As her fighter sped through space, she was pushed back into her seat. She stayed tight on one Gek'Dragar ship and circled around. Red laser fire streaked past her. She threw her fighter into a rolling turn.

When she pulled out, she flew in behind the Gek'Dragar.

She pulled the trigger.

It was a hit. Sparks exploded, and the ship spun sideways.

"Two down," she said. "I have one left."

"I got one. The other two disappeared into the nebula." There was an edge to Kaden's voice. "It's interfering with scanners. I can't see them."

Nea saw her final foe speeding toward the nebula as well. The colored gases swallowed him. The blip on her screen winked out.

She cursed, they were running blind. They couldn't

let them get away.

She saw Kaden flying toward her. "Kaden, I think—"

Suddenly, two Gek'Dragar ships appeared. She shot forward.

"Nea, it's a trap," Kaden yelled.

What?

Seconds later, the third Gek'Dragar ship arrowed out of the nebula at blinding speed, aiming right for her.

It fired and every muscle in her body tensed.

It wasn't a laser. A green cloud engulfed her ship.

She frowned. Alarms started blaring in her cockpit. "Kaden, I've been hit with some sort of—" she tapped her screen "—*gul*, it's a biological agent and it's eating into the ship." She switched one screen to a camera on the hull, and saw holes appearing. "My weapons are offline!"

"Use an electrical pulse." His voice was strong and steady. "It should kill most of whatever it is."

Her fingers danced over the controls. "Okay, I—" Her head jerked up.

The other two Gek'Dragar ships were rushing straight at her, and she could see their weapons were hot.

Her gut clenched. "Kaden—"

"I've got you, Nea."

All of a sudden, the other Terran fighter flew in blindingly fast from the side. Laser fire lit up the space around them. She saw the ship that had sprayed the bio agent on her disintegrate.

Then Kaden's ship clipped one of the other Gek'-Dragar ships.

Nea gasped. No. *No.*

The hit Gek'Dragar ship careened into the final ship.

They both exploded.

She saw the explosion engulf Kaden's ship. A heartbeat later, his ship blew up, as well.

Nea sat in her seat frozen. *No. Kaden.*

A hundred conflicting emotions hit her. Knighthunter Kaden Galath was larger-than-life. He was a force to be reckoned with. He couldn't be...

"Kaden? *Kaden?*"

He couldn't be gone. He was such an intense force. A knot formed in the center of Nea's chest. She stared at the debris, her fingers numb.

"Nea?"

She jolted. His voice came over the console and she blinked. "Kaden?"

"I ejected just in time. Pick me up. Oh, and you owe me. I just saved your life."

She heard his smugness just fine.

She blew out a breath. Alive and as infuriating as ever. She lifted her shaking hands to the controls.

And that's when the thought hit her. Kaden was an excellent pilot. There was no way his ship clipped the Gek'Dragar accidentally.

That meant...he'd done it on purpose.

———

CLAD IN HIS BLACK ARMOR, Kaden hung in space. The nebula was very beautiful up close and personal. The debris of the Gek'Dragar ships was nearby. It was a shame to lose his own ship, but worth it to save Nea.

His hand clenched into a fist. It was unacceptable for her to get hurt or killed.

He spotted her fighter heading his way.

The damage from the bio agent was significant. It would need a full decontamination, and a lot of repairs. Chief Engineer Watson wouldn't be happy. He grimaced. He and Nea would need to go through decontamination, as well.

Her fighter pulled up close—their gazes met through the cockpit canopy.

Ah, she was angry. He hid his smile. She was even more attractive when she was mad. He used his armor to propel over. He gripped the side of the ship.

"I'm on," he said using his implant's comm line.

The ship started forward. She kept the speed low.

"Are you injured?" Her voice was tight.

"No. Any word from the *Helios*?"

"The engines are back online. The stealth generator should be back up soon. The chief is pissed that you blew up her fighter."

He grunted.

"It was reckless, Kaden. You could've been killed." Her tone was clipped.

"Worried about me?"

"Worried that you just rush in, take risks without thinking, and—"

"I thought it through."

She went quiet for a moment. "You hit the Gek'-Dragar ship on purpose."

Now it was his turn to stay silent.

"You saved my life," she said quietly.

The *Helios* appeared ahead.

"Okay, you two." Captain Attaway's voice came clearly across the line. "Leave the ship. We'll tractor it into a containment field. You two come in through airlock four. It'll lead you straight into the decon chamber."

Nea stopped her ship. She activated her armor and retracted the canopy. She floated out, then moved straight past him, heading toward the *Helios*. He followed her toward airlock four. The name was stamped into the metal.

Kaden watched the lock cycle, and then the round door slid open.

Nea flew into the small space, and he followed her. The door closed, and the decontamination chamber re-pressurized.

A moment later Kaden retracted his armor, and Nea did the same. It left them both in the lightweight flight suits.

"All right." Ensign Noth's voice came from the panel. "You guys need to strip. Everything. The cycle takes a few minutes. Have fun."

The young ensign sounded way too cheery. Kaden unfastened his flight suit and shucked it off, then straightened.

Just in time to see Nea push her suit off, leaving her naked.

His gut contracted. He'd imagined her naked numerous times, but the reality was a hundred times better. The overhead lights turned blue, washing over them.

Her breasts were full, tipped with dark pink nipples.

She nipped in at the waist, then her hips flared out. She had strong, toned legs.

She was his perfect idea of a woman.

"Looking your fill, Knighthunter?" Her tone was dry as dust.

He flicked his gaze up to find her glaring at him.

He smiled. "You're worth a long look."

She growled.

"You can look at me all you want," he said. "Fair is fair."

"No, thanks." She sat on the low bench in the center of the space and crossed her legs. A light spray from the decontamination cycle misted over them.

"You're still mad." He walked closer, and battled for control of his cock.

"Yes." She looked up at him. She was being very careful not to look below his neck. "You almost got yourself killed."

He cocked his head. "Would that bother you, Nea?"

She made a scoffing sound and looked away. "You're good at your job. It would be a loss to the Knightforce."

Hmm. He leaned against the wall and crossed his arms. It was hard to keep his cock from rising while they were both naked, and she was sitting there like a queen.

"Well, it would bother me if you get hurt or killed," he said. "That's why I did what I did out there."

Her head whipped around. Then her gaze dropped.

Gul. His gut tightened. It felt like she'd touched him.

Her gaze lingered on his abs, then lowered. He lost the fight, his cock lengthening. He saw her eyes widen and she quickly looked up.

"You hate me," she said.

"I've never hated you."

She shot to her feet and closed the distance between them. "At the Academy, you taunted me, were rude to me, embarrassed me."

"I was a teenage boy. One who'd never...had good role models. I was..."

"An asshole."

It was clear she liked the Terran word. "I was." He paused. "I often still am." He couldn't stop looking at her. She was right there, naked, proud.

"Rude, arrogant, overconfident." She ticked them off on her fingers.

His lips quirked. "You already knew all of this." He managed to pull his gaze off her high, round breasts. "Back then, I knew you, the great Nea Laurier from the grand Laurier family, were way out of my league. You were a reminder that I was nothing."

Her brow creased. "You were mean. Sometimes a bully. You still are." She cocked an eyebrow. "Another Earth word that works is a dick. It means cock, as well as a man who's stupid and rude. It suits you." She stepped closer.

Gul, he could smell her, just about feel the heat of her. Desire was lightning in his blood. She could hardly miss his rock-hard cock.

She smiled. "Looks like your dick is doing its best to rise to the occasion and prove the point."

Before he knew what she had planned, she reached out and wrapped her hand around his cock.

Kaden jerked and a harsh sound escaped him.

She squeezed. "I know you mustn't be an asshole all the time, or Ashtin wouldn't be your best friend."

The last thing Kaden wanted to talk about when Nea had her hand on his cock was his best friend. "Like what you're touching, Nea? Have you thought about it before? How good it would feel sliding inside you?"

She gasped.

He reached out and touched her nipple. It was already a tight bud.

Suddenly, the decon cycle ended. The lights blinked on.

Nea blinked, then released him and stepped back. Her chest heaved.

Then she swiveled, snatched a plain-white robe off a hook on the wall, and yanked it on. She strode out of the room.

CHAPTER FIVE

What the *gul* had she been thinking?

She *hadn't* been thinking.

Nea strode out of the decon chamber and into the dressing area. Extra spacesuits were hanging on hooks, and a storage room off to the side was filled with crates of gear.

She'd touched Kaden Galath.

Right now, her body was trembling, alive with sensation where he'd touched her.

And she'd wrapped her hand around his very long, hard cock.

"Nea."

His voice shivered through her. She spun. He'd wrapped a towel around his hips. His skin was pale and stretched over hard muscles. His abs were all hard ridges, and his chest... The man had a perfect chest.

I never hated you.

It would bother me if you got killed.

That's why I did what I did.

"Tell me you don't want me."

His dark voice wrapped around her, and her belly kicked.

He took a step closer. "Tell me you didn't like my cock in your hand."

She sucked in a breath and glared at him. "I don't like you."

"But you want me."

She shoved against his chest. "You are the most infuriating man I've ever known."

He kept staring.

"You're arrogant, abrupt, rude." All the emotion inside her roiled like a furious storm. Her head told her to get out of there... But the rest of her wasn't listening.

Some part of her did want him.

Nea was all about her work as a knight. It was who she was to the very fiber of her being. She never did things just for fun, for enjoyment. She never did what she wanted. She did what was best for the Knightforce, for Oronis, for her father and living up to the Laurier name.

She'd almost died today. Kaden had almost died.

Instead of stepping away from him, she stepped closer, then she shrugged off her robe. It slithered off her, leaving her naked.

And she had the glorious moment of seeing Kaden Galath shocked.

She was burning up. She kept thinking of the moment when his ship had exploded.

And now, she wasn't going to think. She wasn't going to follow the rules. No, for once in her life, she was just going to feel.

She met his gaze. "Don't think this means I like you, Galath."

His gaze flared. "Noted."

Then he lowered his head and pressed his mouth to hers.

She made a sound, and he yanked her closer. She slid her hands roughly into his platinum hair and kissed him back. Of course, he could kiss well, and he tasted so good. Dark spice and dangerous secrets.

His hands skated down her body. She jumped up, and wrapped her legs around his lean waist.

"*Gul.*" He looked dazed. He stumbled into the storage room, and kicked the door closed behind them.

She sucked in a breath at the intense need on his face. No one had ever looked at her like that before. Not sensible, studious Nea Laurier.

He snaked an arm around her, and pushed her back. Her back arched and his gaze locked on her chest.

"These breasts," he said on a groan. "So beautiful. I've fantasized about them."

He had? She couldn't think straight, but when he lowered his head and licked one nipple, she cried out.

He used his lips, his teeth, and tongue. She slid her hands into his pale hair. Desire was growing like a fire— out of control, wild. His clever mouth moved to her other nipple. Oh, stars above.

He backed them up until her ass hit the edge of a crate, the metal cool on her bare skin. He balanced her there, and his hand slid down her thigh.

"I can smell how aroused you are." His voice was lower, huskier. His hand dipped between her thighs.

"Oh..." Nea bit her lip and let her head fall back.

"So wet, Nea. All for me." He slid a finger inside her.

She moaned. When his knuckle hit her most sensitive spot, she couldn't bear it any longer. "No talking. Just fuck me."

Another finger joined the first, stretching her, and she bit her lip hard.

He leaned over her, his mouth on the side of her neck. She felt the scrape of his teeth.

"Who's fucking you, Nea? Say my name."

"Just hurry up." She undulated against him.

"Say it."

She shoved him and growled. "*Galath.*"

"That'll do for now."

Arrogant. She spun and leaned over the crate, challenge in her eyes.

His gaze was on her. "This ass—" he palmed one buttock, then his strong body pressed against hers.

She felt his cock—hot and hard—against her.

"And this is beautiful." His fingers skimmed down her spine, and the ink embedded in her skin.

She flushed. She'd never let anyone see it. "Hurry up."

"I want you to remember this," he murmured. "I know I will."

Her heart hammered. "Can you just—?"

He surged inside her, filling her.

The air rushed out of her lungs, and she made a strangled sound. The way he filled her... She felt full, stretched. By the *gul*-vexed stars, Kaden was inside her.

He leaned over her, covering her. His hot skin

pressed against hers, and he nipped her earlobe. She fought back a moan.

"I can't wait to hear you scream my name," he whispered hotly.

He pulled out, and plunged back in. Heat rocked through her.

She gripped the crate. "I'm not screaming yet, Kaden."

He chuckled, and found a hard, powerful rhythm.

She bit her lip, feeling tossed around by all the sensations. A small cry broke free of her lips.

"So tight. I knew this would be so..."

He didn't finish and she desperately wanted to know. She pushed back against him, feeling out of control, desperate. His flesh slapped against hers. His ragged breathing was loud in the small room. He was just as affected as she was.

His hand slid under her body and found the tight bundle of nerves above her sex. "I can't wait to feel you come for me."

Oh. *Oh.* Before she could brace herself, her orgasm hit, and her muscles clenched.

"*Kaden.*" She was drenched in hot pleasure. She'd never felt anything so strong.

He pumped into her hard, and let out a low roar. She felt him shudder, his release filling her.

She stilled, trying to catch her breath. She'd just had the best sex of her life. With Kaden Galath.

Kaden Galath's release was leaking down her thighs.

What had she done?

He slammed a hand down on the crate beside her head, his breathing harsh.

He'd poked, prodded, and challenged her. She'd liked it. All of it.

Panic slithered through her. She elbowed him and slipped sideways. She couldn't look at him.

"Nea—"

She shook her head. She needed to regroup. At least their combat implants kept them safe from diseases and provided contraceptives.

Dredging up the strength to keep her emotions off her face, she lifted her chin. "This never happened. It changes nothing."

She stalked out.

IN HIS CABIN, Kaden pulled on some clothes. His usual all black.

He stopped, pressed a hand to his hip, then blew out a breath.

He couldn't stop thinking about Nea. Remembering every single detail of her body, the sounds she'd made for him, the heat and challenge in her eyes, and how it felt to slide inside her.

With a groan, he pressed a palm to his throbbing cock.

He wanted to feel the tight clench of her again. Hear her cry his name.

Gul.

He shoved a hand through his hair. He'd been

obsessed with her for as long as he could remember. At first, he'd been in awe. She was practically an Oronis princess. A part of him, a dark part that had always been alone, wanted her. Desperately.

Kaden closed his eyes. He kept that dark part locked up. It was twisted up with his different abilities. He knew his energy was different to most knights. More dangerous, harder to control, always hungry to be used.

A memory from the Academy hit him.

Kaden strode across the Academy Courtyard. He was late for his next class. But when his gaze snagged on the girl sitting by the central fountain, comp pad in hand, her brow furrowed as she read, he slowed down.

Nea Laurier.

His chest tightened. He changed direction and forgot all about his class.

She'd be studying for some test. Nea was always studying.

Stars, she was beautiful. Not in the soft, delicate way of some girls. Her features were stronger, a little tougher. He liked them way better. As he got closer, he noted her thick, black hair and wondered how silky it was.

Her head snapped up.

"Nose in a book again, Laurier," he said.

He saw her shoulders stiffen. He hated that.

"Carry on, Galath. I don't have time for you today."

He stopped right beside her, leg brushing her knee. She stiffened even more. He peered at the book and snorted. "You probably have that memorized already. Why not give the studying a rest, relax, live a little?"

She glared at him with her pretty aqua-blue eyes. "Go away."

Her skin was a deep honey color and he desperately wanted to stroke it. He wished he could sit with her in the sunshine, make her laugh.

Kaden's insides twisted. He felt the darkness inside him, one he'd grown up with, one that twisted his energy. He'd always known he was different. He'd been born in the gutter, abandoned by his parents, raised in a care home. He was no one, nothing, and he fought daily to not let the darkness win.

And he would never, ever let it touch Nea.

"Surprised you aren't in the library." He let his lips curl. "Pretty sure your seat in there has the shape of your ass molded into it."

She sucked in a sharp breath, and he thought he saw her quickly hide a flash of hurt. His stomach knotted.

Do what you have to do to keep her safe, Galath. He had to remember that.

Sensing a presence, he looked over her shoulder. This time, he stiffened.

Her father stood nearby, glaring at Kaden.

"I'll see you around, Laurier." He stalked off, straight toward Torquin Laurier.

"I'll never understand why they let no-name scum like you into the Academy," the older man said quietly.

Ah, well at least the man was consistent. He always said some version of those words when he saw Kaden. Of course, he was careful never to let anyone overhear him.

Laurier's face twisted. "You sully the halls here just by

breathing. You with the name they assigned you at the care home."

"Good to see you too, sir." Kaden met Laurier's gaze and held it. "It's always a pleasure."

"Stay away from my daughter."

Kaden just kept staring. He lifted a hand, and let a pulse of red energy flicker over his fingers. He was gratified to see a flicker of uneasiness in the older man before the older man shouldered past and headed for Nea.

With a blink, Kaden came back to the present. He blew out another breath and yanked his shirt on.

He'd fucked Nea. It had been great. It should've gotten her out of his system. Ended this fascination.

He lifted his head and stared at his face in the mirror.

How could he never touch her again? The desire and need now seemed a whole lot worse.

You have a mission, Galath.

Knighthunters were encouraged not to form attachments. They were purposely selected to become knighthunters because they had no strong family ties. And he knew it was best for a man like him.

His trainers would not be happy about his feelings for Nea Laurier.

Nor would her father.

Kaden scowled. Torquin Laurier was an overbearing, self-important idiot. Even to this day, he made it clear he thought Kaden wasn't worthy—to be a knight, or to be breathing the same air as his daughter.

Still, the man seemed to love her.

Kaden headed out of his cabin, and did a quick check

in on the bridge. He found Ensign Noth and Chief Engineer Watson hunched over a console.

"The engines?" he asked.

"Purring like a satisfied cat." The chief frowned. "Do you have cats on Oron?"

He smiled. "We have felines."

Chief Watson nodded. "You and the knightmaster did a good job out there, but you blew up my fighter."

"Technically, the Gek'Dragar did it."

The woman made an unhappy noise. "And you got the other one half chewed up."

He spread his hands. "Gek'Dragar again."

The ensign was trying to hide a grin.

The chief's gaze narrowed. "You have an answer for everything."

Kaden winked at her.

She shook her head and mumbled about incorrigible men.

"So, do you anticipate any more problems?" he asked.

"Everything is running within parameters, but like I said, the stealth generator is untested. We've never run it this long. Anything could happen."

He slid his hands into his pockets. "But we'll have no trouble tracking the knightqueen's ship?"

"No. It's headed deeper into Gek'Dragar space."

Silence fell. They all knew that it made things exponentially more dangerous.

"Well, I'll leave you to it." He paused. "Have you seen Knightmaster Nea?"

"She's in her cabin," the ensign replied.

Kaden nodded.

"You think you're fooling anyone?"

He glanced at the chief engineer. "Excuse me?"

"I've seen the way you look at the knightmaster when she isn't looking at you."

For the first time in years, Kaden fought the urge to squirm. "And how's that?"

The older woman smiled. "I'm old, but I'm not too old to see when a man has it bad. You look at her like she's the most delicious dessert you can't wait to devour."

Gul. He was usually better at hiding his thoughts and feelings. He didn't respond; just turned to leave.

"Kaden?"

He glanced back.

"She looks at you, too," the chief said.

He held the engineer's gaze for a second, then strode out.

Yes, Nea looked at him like she'd enjoy skewering him with her sword. He made his way toward the galley. They'd all been using the *Helios'* food printers to eat from, since no kitchen staff had been allowed on this mission.

Did Nea really look at him? Without hate and annoyance?

He grabbed a tray and started replicating some Oronis food that he'd inputted into the computer system. He ate a few things, his mind dwelling on thoughts of Nea.

She had a tattoo along her spine.

That had been a surprise when she'd turned that sexy, naked back toward him. They were Oronis roses with thorns. A sign of strength and tenacity.

He wished he'd had time to explore them.

Tattoos were not common on Oron, especially among the elite families. They were usually seen as things commoners did.

The knightmaster had a secret rebellious streak.

He'd bet pure wesium metal that her father didn't know.

Inspiration struck, and he moved back to the replicator, pushing the button to prime the machine.

The food printer beeped. He set a dish on the tray. He replicated some tala. The fruit was deliciously sweet and tart. Nea had a slight addiction to it, but tala were notoriously difficult to get. They only grew for two months of the year, in a certain climate. And replicators didn't always do them justice. He tested one and nodded. The food printers on the *Helios* had done a good job.

He set the red-and-yellow fruit on the dish. He'd sometimes left tala for Nea at the Academy—on her desk, in her room, in her locker. She'd never discovered it was him. He'd be the last person she would've guessed.

He carried the tray down the corridor, and stopped at the door to her cabin.

The urge to knock was enormous. He wanted to see her, hear her voice.

Who was he kidding? He wanted to touch her again. If he went in there, he wanted her naked again, and crying out for him as she came.

He dragged in a deep breath.and set the tray down. He was a corridor away when he used his implant to ring her door chime.

CHAPTER SIX

"Argh." Nea landed a flurry of punches and kicks to the exercise bag in the *Helios* gym.

She'd been at it for a while. Her sports top was damp with sweat. She hadn't slept well. Her body had been itchy, alive.

Wanting more sex.

More Kaden.

Her next kick set the bag rocking.

She paused, chest heaving. Memories assailed her. Her hands gripping the crate as Kaden powered inside her, his fingers touching her right where she needed it.

No. Not happening again.

She had a mission. An extremely important one.

She swiped her arm across her forehead. She'd found a tray of food outside her cabin last night. She hadn't asked the *Helios* crew if they'd left it. Mainly because she didn't want to hear that it was from him.

It contained all her favorite foods. How had he known?

He's a knighthunter, remember? Uncovering information was his trade. There'd been tala fruit on the tray. Her favorite. She'd had an admirer at the Academy who used to leave them for her. She'd waited for him to make a move and ask her out, but he never had, much to her disappointment.

The mysterious stranger had gone to a lot of effort to give her that fruit for several years.

Could Kaden have—?

No. It couldn't have been him.

Her implant chimed in her head with an incoming message.

Knightmaster, Captain Attaway needs you on the bridge.

She replied.

On my way.

She found a towel and wiped her face. She slung it around her neck and then hurried to the bridge. The doors opened, and the first thing she saw was Kaden.

Her body lit up.

She gritted her teeth. *Gul*-vexed stars, he looked perfect. Standing tall, black clothing accenting his lean, muscled body, not a strand of platinum hair out of place.

Meanwhile she was a sweaty, hot mess.

He turned his head and stared at her with an unblinking, blue gaze.

She forced herself to look at Captain Attaway. "What's going on?"

The captain pointed at the viewscreen. A large, pale-yellow orb filled the space.

"This is Solari," Kaden said. "A desert planet in Gek'-Dragar space, but the native species are the Solarians. A very distant relative of the Gek'Dragar. They're impoverished. The Gek'Dragar give them limited support, and they also ravaged the planet for centuries, mining all the once-vast deposits of metal and minerals."

"The scans confirm that," the ensign said. "It likely once had a temperate climate, but over-mining and no rehabilitation afterward turned the climate hotter and drier. Then the deserts formed."

"Okay," Nea said. "Why are we interested in Solari?"

"The ship carrying the knightqueen landed here," Kaden said.

Nea straightened and frowned. "Why? I would have presumed they were taking her to one of the central Gek'-Dragar planets."

"We detected hyon radiation in their trail," Chief Watson said. "My guess, they're having engine troubles."

"We think they landed to make repairs," Kaden said.

Nea's pulse quickened. Knightqueen Carys could be down there. "We need to get down there."

Kaden nodded.

"Take shuttle three," the captain said. "It has some land speeders aboard as well, if you need ground transport. Good luck."

NEA LET Kaden pilot the shuttle. They'd left the Helios, and their ship was aiming straight at Solari.

As they got closer, she could see bands of colors crossing the deserts—yellow, beige, white, and brown. She didn't see any green or blue.

Her lips pressed together. Curse the Gek'Dragar.

There was an uneasy tension in the cockpit that she was trying to ignore. Her hands clenched on the porta-comp in her lap.

"You didn't even fight me for the pilot seat," Kaden said lightly. "I'm disappointed."

"You're the better pilot." It grated to admit it, but it was true.

"Barely."

She kept her gaze on the porta-comp. She'd loaded up all the information on Solari and its people. They had the landing location of the Gek'Dragar ship loaded into the shuttle computer. The plan was to land nearby, then go in on speeders.

"Are you ever going to look at me?"

She glanced at him, then back at the screen. "If you're looking for a replay of...earlier, it's not happening."

"It's going to happen."

That over-confident tone lit a fuse. "You arrogant *gul*—"

"It's happening, Nea, because we're both still thinking about it. I bet you're wet right now. I know I'm half hard."

Nea hissed, and barely resisted pressing her thighs together to dull the throb. "I hate you."

The *gul* just smiled at her.

She looked straight ahead, just as they hit the atmosphere.

Kaden flew in low over the desert. It was a washed-out, yellowish-white. All sand and dust, with no vegetation. Stark and desolate.

"It's hard to imagine this was ever green," she murmured.

"Yes. Look."

They flew over an area of deep holes. An abandoned mine.

Steps were cut deep into the landscape. It wasn't the careful mining the Oronis did. Not safe extraction of resources, with intensive rehabilitation of the land afterward. This looked unplanned and haphazard. Just greedy destruction.

They kept flying. There were more mined-out areas, and more dust-dry desert.

"We'll land by that ridge," Kaden said.

Nea studied the outcropping. The rocks were a darker brown, and several rock formations cast interesting silhouettes against the sky.

"The location where the Gek'Dragar ship landed is on the other side. The *Helios* scan indicated a small outpost."

She nodded.

Please let the knightqueen be here.

KADEN KICKED THE LAND SPEEDER.

His boot made a dull *thunk*. He landed another kick,

denting the metal side panel. *Better.* He'd already smeared both speeders with dust and sand. He wanted them to look old, dirty, and well-used. He added some interesting scratches to the side of the other one.

Stepping back, in the small cargo bay of the shuttle, he put his hands on his hips. He could almost hear Chief Watson cursing him.

The speeders looked the part now. He and Nea would be pretending to be prospectors, picking over the abandoned mines. That was common on Solari. People came here looking for remnants of berillo. The ore was still commonly used throughout the universe.

Nea stepped through the doorway from the cockpit. She was dressed in brown leather pants that hugged her body, a beige-colored shirt, and she had a green, light-weight scarf wrapped around her neck and goggles resting up on her forehead.

Apart from her straight bearing, she looked every bit the adventurer. Kaden's outfit was similar to hers, except he had a leather vest over his shirt.

They'd both attached fake ridges on their cheeks as a disguise. The adhesive itched, but he was used to disguises; they were part of the life of a knighthunter.

"Ready?" he asked.

She nodded and eyed the speeders. "The chief is going to gut you when we get back."

"I'm sure I can sweet talk her."

"No doubt."

Nea swung a leg over her speeder and started it up. A moment later, it lifted off the ground, hovering, before she rode down the ramp.

Kaden started his speeder, the engine purring like a desert cat. He followed, activating the security system on the shuttle via his implant.

Hot air hit his face as they raced across a salt flat. He glanced to the left. Nea was keeping pace beside him. She leaned forward over her scratched-up speeder.

His body tightened. He'd been fighting his obsession for her for a long time, and it seemed to be a losing battle. He watched her dark hair stream behind her. Being with her, being inside her, pleasuring her had made everything worse.

His control was eroding, and he wasn't sure he could get a grip on it.

He forced his gaze off her and spotted the outpost in the distance ahead.

Nea's message pinged through his implant.

We're almost there.

Acknowledged.

He forced himself to focus on the mission.

They swept into the outpost. It was dusty, with a few single-story, stone dwellings. Some were rectangular, others domed shaped. Many had fabric awnings and flags, fluttering in the hot wind.

There was a small junkyard to one side of the outpost. Kaden saw the Gek'Dragar ship parked nearby, and his pulse kicked.

They were close. The knightqueen and Sten could still be here.

Kaden and Nea pulled their speeders to a halt near a few others in a small, fenced-in area.

Nea whipped her scarf over her dusty hair. The ridges of her disguise accented her features and her aristocratic face.

"Ready?" she asked.

"Ready."

They headed toward the only tavern. Several locals watched them—wary and suspicious.

The tavern was located near the small junkyard and attached repair shop. Several junk parts were stacked outside the shop, along with an old freighter, half pulled to bits. Faded, red flags slapped in the breeze above the shop.

They reached the tavern and took a seat at one of the small tables under the awnings. An older Solarian man ambled over. He had gray, scaled skin like a Gek'Dragar, but no tail and a slimmer build. He had two black horns sweeping back from his face.

"Help ya?"

"Two drinks," Kaden said. "Whatever you have that's good, as long as it's cold."

The man grunted and waved at a serving droid. "You're not from around here."

"Nope." Kaden leaned back in his chair.

"We're prospectors," Nea said. "Thirsty ones."

The man grunted again. With a whir of gears, the boxy droid rolled over, bringing them two foamy ales.

"We might need some parts," Kaden said. "One of our speeder engines is playing up."

The man stroked his graying beard. "Then you need

Poc." He pointed a thumb at the repair shop and attached shipyard. "Only guy in town. He might have what you need."

"Thanks." Kaden sipped his drink.

"Prospectors from where?" the man continued.

Nea lifted her glass. "Pharad."

Kaden reached out and toyed with her hair. She glared at him.

"But my love and I travel around. As long as we're together, we're happy."

The tavern owner sniffed. "The berillo is played out here. You won't find much." He lowered his voice. "I also recommend you steer clear of the Gek'Dragar."

Kaden raised his glass. "Thanks. Never been fond of them."

With a nod, the man headed back inside.

Nea shoved Kaden's hand away. "Being a couple wasn't a part of our cover."

"It made sense." The ale was weak, but cold. He eyed the repair shop and shipyard over her shoulder. "Finish your drink, my sweet star. Then we need to get on board that Gek'Dragar ship."

Nea nodded and lifted her glass.

They finished their drinks and paid. They casually walked toward the repair shop. As they neared, the clanging of some tool on metal reverberated through the still air. The building was open-air, with a roof made of tattered fabric, and no walls. As Kaden stepped into the shade, Nea wandered off, as though she were studying the parts and junk.

"Hello?" he called.

The clanging stopped. A figure approached. He was Brisid, with a stocky body, rough, brown skin, and four arms. A Solarian boy, probably mid-teens, hovered nearby. His black horns were short and slender.

The Brisid wiped all four hands on some rags. "You lost?"

"Not if you're Poc," Kaden said. "We're prospectors. We need a transition coil. Our speeder engine is playing up."

Poc eyed him. "I might have something."

I'm entering the ship.

The message from Nea pinged across his comm line.

That meant Kaden needed to keep Poc busy.

Any Gek'Dragar?

None that I can see.

Kaden followed Poc over to some metal crates. He saw the boy glancing at the Gek'Dragar ship.

Gul. Had he seen Nea?

"You the apprentice?" Kaden asked.

The boy looked back at him and nodded. "Not much else to do around here."

"Be thankful for any work, boy." Poc lifted several parts out of a crate.

"That a Gek'Dragar ship?" Kaden asked.

Poc stiffened a little. "Yeah."

"Looks like it's in good condition."

"It just landed," the boy said.

His boss shot him a sharp look. "Quiet." He held up a part. "Here. Pay and get gone."

The ship's empty, Kaden.

He heard her frustration in those few short words.

Okay. Get out. They can't have taken Queen Carys far. We'll ask around. Someone had to have seen something.

Kaden paid for the part. "So is the Gek'Dragar ship for sale?"

"No." Poc turned and walked away.

The boy looked like he was about to say more, but a look from Poc had him clamping his mouth shut.

Kaden lifted the part. "Thanks. May your water be plentiful."

At the common Solari phrase, Poc jerked his chin up.

Kaden turned and saw Nea waiting for him in the shade of a nearby building.

Their next step would be finding someone willing to talk to them.

CHAPTER SEVEN

Nea watched Kaden stride across the outpost.

By the stars, the man had a loose-hipped stride that made a woman take notice. Even wearing dusty desert gear, with leather clinging to his muscular legs, he was eye-catching.

Pulling her eyes off his body, she followed him. They both made their way slowly down the street. The locals either looked away, or ignored them.

"No sign of Carys or Sten," Kaden said quietly.

She shook her head, her stomach knotted. She had desperately wanted the knightqueen to be here, somewhere.

"It looked like the engine had been opened up on the Gek'Dragar ship," Nea said. "But Poc wasn't working on it."

Kaden scanned the outpost. "There's no sign another ship left here. Where the *gul* did they take her?"

"We need to ask around," she said. "Someone must have seen her."

"These people were crushed under Gek'Dragar rule. They're wary, and distrust strangers."

"We have to get them talking," she said. "Let's split up."

Kaden looked like he wanted to argue, but he finally gave her a brusque nod.

Nea pulled her scarf over her head. She wandered down the street. She saw two old men in tattered clothes playing a game of some sort on a battered board.

"Hello," she said.

They eyed her. One had a twisted scar on his face, and one of his horns was snapped off. He looked like he'd been attacked by a wild animal a long time ago.

"No one likes strangers around here." The scarred man's voice was raspy. "Best be on your way."

"My partner and I are prospectors. Do you have any good information on mines for us to hit? I'll pay."

The other man was tall and thin, and his gray skin was very pale. He rocked his stool back on two legs. "The Gek'Dragar left nothing. We have no information for you."

"I can really make it worth your while—"

"Girl, see my face?" The scarred one glared at her. "This is what happens if you ask too many questions."

"Who did that to you?" she asked quietly.

"Gek'Dragar. They destroyed everything on this planet. Now, go." He spat onto the sand, like he was ridding himself of a bad taste.

She looked around. "The Gek'Dragar still here? I thought they left Solari when the mines ran dry."

"They never truly leave." The thin man shook his head.

Both men looked back at their game, ignoring her.

They never truly leave. That meant the Gek'Dragar still had a presence on Solari. Turning it over in her head, she continued through the outpost.

She heard the bellow of an animal. As she turned a corner, she came upon a pen full of shaggy animals. They were big and hairy, with long horns. Her implants said they were a native species called the *kuvox*. They were designed for the desert, and needed little water. Their brown fur recycled their sweat to help retain water.

She wondered how Kaden was getting on. The kuvox shifted, restlessly, and she spotted a tall, muscular Solari working with the animals.

She leaned on the fence and watched. She pushed her scarf back. One young kuvox pranced, ignoring the man's instructions. She laughed quietly.

The man glanced over. His wide-brimmed hat shaded his face and covered his horns. "Don't encourage him."

She held her hands up.

The man walked over, eyeing her. She saw the spark of appreciation in his dark eyes.

"Looks like you have your hands full," she said.

"I always do. Kuvox can be stubborn. I'm Vark."

"Nea."

"That's a pretty name. What are you doing in a hell-hole like this, Nea?"

"My partner and I are prospectors."

"Ah. Picking over the mines. There's not much to be found."

"So I'm told." She paused. "I heard that there are still Gek'Dragar around."

Vark tensed for a second, but didn't look away. "Yeah. Best not to run into them."

"Any place in particular that I should avoid?"

"Yes." He stepped closer to the fence. His features were quite pleasant, and his weathered, gray skin suited him. "How about I buy you a drink at the tavern, pretty Nea?"

"Oh, well—"

"She's not available for a drink."

Nea barely controlled her jolt. How had he snuck up on her like that?

A strong arm snaked around her middle, and pulled her back against that long, muscular body.

Gul. She couldn't pull away and risk their cover.

"Kaden, this is Vark. Vark, this is my partner."

"Maybe we'll get that drink another time, Nea." Vark resettled his hat on his head.

"Or not," Kaden said darkly.

The idiot. She could have gotten more information from Vark, if he hadn't interfered.

The animal handler nodded, then ambled back toward his animals.

"He was going to talk," she whispered hotly. "You ruined the chance."

"He wanted you naked, not talking." Kaden took her hand and towed her across the outpost.

"Kaden—"

They turned a corner, and all of a sudden, he pushed her against the wall. She gasped. His body pinned hers to the warm stone. He was all heat and hard muscle.

"No one imagines you naked but me." His mouth hovered over hers.

Her belly clenched and she cursed her traitorous body. Liquid heat ran through her veins.

"No one touches you but me," he said.

Then he kissed her.

It was hard, and hotter than the desert. His tongue tangled with hers.

Nea wanted to moan, and instead kissed him back. She stroked her tongue against his.

It was the nervous sound of a throat clearing that broke the kiss.

Nea shoved Kaden and he stepped back. His face looked carved from stone, his ice-blue eyes alive with heat.

She looked past him, and saw the teen boy from the shipyard. He shifted his feet, touching one of his horns and looking nervous.

IT WAS hard for Kaden to pull away from Nea. Her body ignited him. Usually, he always felt cool and in control.

Except with her.

She lit him up, right down to the depths of the darkest parts of his soul.

He forced himself to spin and face the boy. Under his stare, the boy wilted.

"Kaden." Nea elbowed him. "You're scaring him."

"I'm not afraid." The teenager's chin jutted out.

Kaden fought a smile. The kid reminded him of himself. "You have something for us?"

Nea huffed. "What's your name?"

"Tolo." He flicked a glance at Kaden, before focusing on Nea. "Are you here to help her?"

Both Kaden and Nea stiffened.

"Help who?" Nea asked.

"The beautiful woman." The boy licked his lips. "They tried to hide her, but I saw her. Her hair was like gold. She was so beautiful. Like the brightest sun." There was awe in the boy's voice.

"We're here to save her," Nea said. "Who's they? Who had her?"

"The Gek'Dragar." The teen's nose wrinkled. "Those sand lickers are—" he cut off and looked around, then he swallowed. "They ruin everything. They kill, take what isn't theirs."

"They are no friends of ours," Nea told him. "Do you know where they took the woman?"

The teenager gave a brief nod. "Their ship will take time to get fixed. They were angry with Poc. They didn't want to wait."

Kaden felt a prickle on the back of his neck. He glanced around and gestured deeper into the shade between two buildings. He didn't want to get the boy killed if he was spotted talking with them.

"They needed another ship," Kaden said.

The boy nodded.

"Where?" Kaden asked. "Where did they take her?"

"The old Gek'Dragar mining base. It isn't too far away from here. It's buried in the Omhos Ridge. It was the head of all the mining operations here. They ran all security out of there, too. Most of the Gek'Dragar left after the mines finished, but there's a small garrison still stationed there." Tolo plucked at his clothes. "They come into town sometimes. They expect food and drink, and they never pay." He got a belligerent look. "The woman looked too nice to be with them. There was a man with her, but he was beaten up. If it hurts the Gek to lose them, and that woman is safe..." The boy pulled in a breath. "No one deserves to be the Gek'Dragar's prisoner." Now raw grief crossed his face. "My father was. They killed him."

Kaden nodded. "We'll get her back. Where's the base exactly? How do we get there?"

The kid proved to be a fountain of intel. He quickly drew them a map and shared several landmarks to get to the base.

"Thank you." Nea touched the boy's shoulder.

Tolo nodded.

"Now go," Kaden said. "Before your boss notices you missing."

The teen took a step, then hesitated. "Good luck." He hurried away.

They had a location, and a basic external layout of the base.

Kaden frowned. It wasn't much, but it was something. "We have no idea of the Gek'Dragar numbers, or the internal layout of the base."

"It's enough," Nea said. "She's here, Kaden. We need to get her now."

"We'll be going in blind."

They headed back toward their speeders.

Nea arched a brow "I'm sure you've been in far tighter spots, and gone in with less."

He scowled. He'd often done that, but not with Nea at his side. He flexed his hand.

"Kaden?"

He looked at her.

"We've got this," she said. "Our duty is to our queen."

He nodded. The knightqueen was the heart of the Oronis. They had to save her.

He threw a leg over his speeder and started it up. Beside him, Nea revved hers. They headed out of the outpost, a cloud of dust rising behind them.

It wouldn't be a short trip. First, they had to reach the base across harsh, desert terrain. Then they needed to get close enough to confirm the knightqueen was there without alerting the Gek'Dragar.

He activated his implant. "Kaden to the *Helios*."

"*Helios* here, Kaden." It was Ensign Noth.

"Have any ships left this area?"

"Negative. And none will be any time soon."

Kaden frowned. "Why?"

"An ion storm moved into the upper atmosphere. Makes it dangerous for ships to leave. It's not scheduled to clear until tomorrow."

A small break. "We believe Knightqueen Carys and

her knightguard are being held at an old Gek'Dragar base. We think they're looking to transfer her to another ship. Knightmaster Nea and I are investigating."

"Kaden, you believe she's still on the planet?" Captain Attaway said across the line.

"We hope so."

"Captain, can you scan the base?" Nea asked. "Give us any additional intel."

"Negative." The ensign sounded apologetic. "The remnants of berillo ore in the rock render our scans useless."

Kaden muttered a curse. "We'll get closer and see what's happening at that base."

"Be careful, Kaden," the captain said.

"Always."

The captain laughed. "I don't believe that for a second. Good luck."

He and Nea raced across a flat, dusty plane. Ahead, he saw a large mountain range, with one part of it covered in mining terraces. A canyon that cut through it. Tolo had told them about it. It was the quickest way to the other side.

They slowed, and Kaden zoomed into the narrow gap after Nea. They followed the rocky twists and turns. He spotted some goat-like animals that bounded up the side of the sheer cliff face.

Suddenly, he saw Nea's speeder slow down. He pulled in closer.

"Problem?" he asked.

Her brow creased. "There's something wrong with my engine. It's clunking and losing speed."

He scanned ahead. "Let's push on a bit farther. We'll get out of the canyon and then take a look."

She nodded.

Her speeder was moving much more slowly, now, and smoke had started coming out of the back of it.

They finally passed out of the canyon and onto another flat plane. Kaden's implant didn't detect anyone on scanners. At least out here, they'd spot anyone coming who tried to sneak up on them.

He saw something in the distance, and zoomed his vision in. A patch of long, narrow trees, and a glimmer on the ground.

"Looks like there's an oasis ahead. We'll stop there."

Nea babied her smoking speeder along. They limped into the oasis.

She got off and kicked the side of the speeder. "*Gul!*"

"I suspect Terran speeders aren't designed to withstand Solari conditions." He stood. "No ships can leave the planet right now because of the ion storm. We have time."

There was worry in her eyes. "But Carys mightn't."

Kaden gripped Nea's shoulder. "Deep breath. We need some patience, and we're never giving up. Let's look at the speeder."

CHAPTER EIGHT

Nea huffed out a breath and glared at the smoking speeder.

Gul. Gul. Gul. She wanted to reach the base and find the knightqueen.

They couldn't go in on one speeder. If they found Carys and Sten, they needed two speeders to get them out of there.

Kaden pried a panel off her speeder. A wave of heat washed over them. He tried to touch the engine, then yanked his hand back, shaking his fingers.

"Can you tell what's wrong?" she asked.

"It's too hot to tell anything right now. We'll need to wait for it cool down."

She gritted her teeth. More waiting.

He shook his head, a faint smile on his lips. "Go, explore the oasis. Do something."

"Do what?" She glanced over her shoulder. She reluctantly had to admit the oasis was pretty.

There was a clear pool of water, surrounded by long,

straight trees, with thin, dry foliage, giving some shade. Her combat implants had already told her that the water was safe.

Kaden turned and walked toward the pool.

"Where are you going?" she asked.

"I'm going to wash the dust off." He pulled his scarf off and dropped it, then his vest. Next, he pulled his shirt off. "Feel free to join me."

She scowled, staring at the muscles in his back. "I'll scout the perimeter."

Nea spun, but her body felt jittery. She wanted to follow him. She wanted to watch him.

She growled under her breath.

No. She wasn't going there again.

The knightqueen was her only focus. It was so frustrating to be so close, but unable to get to the base.

She glanced at the broken speeder. She prayed to the knights of old that it would cool down fast, so Kaden could fix it.

Behind her, she heard the splash of water. Resolutely, she didn't look in that direction.

She circled the oasis. There was no sign of anyone having been there. There were sparse animal tracks, but that was it.

She glanced out across the dry, harsh landscape. For a second, she got the sense of being totally alone. Far from anything and anyone.

Nea often felt that way, even when she was standing in the middle of a crowded room. At the Academy, she'd never really felt connected to anyone. She'd studied and trained exceptionally hard—as Kaden had always tormented her about. She'd always been conscious that she was a Laurier. Her father had drummed into her the belief that she had to always work harder than anyone else.

She didn't mind. She'd always wanted to be a knight, and she was good at it. She didn't need a pack of friends and acquaintances. Being a knightmaster meant she had to keep some walls up between herself and those under her command. As a leader, she couldn't be their friend, too.

There was the sound of more splashing, and the urge to look was too great. She turned.

Kaden sliced across the pool with fast strokes. His power and athleticism were clear.

Tingles rippled through her entire body. She growled. She needed to get this attraction under control.

She stomped toward the speeders, but could see the shimmer of heat still coming off hers. It was still too hot.

"You're wound too tight."

She glanced at the pool. Kaden was standing waist deep, water sluicing down his hard chest. *Those muscles.* She jerked her eyes to his face.

"I want to find the knightqueen," she said.

"If you go in wound up, you'll make a mistake. You'll get yourself killed."

"I can take care of myself, Galath."

"Come in and cool off. Then we'll take a look at the speeder."

Nea hesitated. The water did look good. After several mental arguments, she unwound her scarf.

She strode over and crouched at the edge of the pool,

then splashed some water on her face. It soaked into her shirt and felt good.

There was no sound, but she lifted her gaze. Kaden, and all his taut muscles and wet skin, was standing close by.

"Come in," he urged.

"No."

"It's hot, and we have time."

She shook her head.

"Afraid?"

"Your taunts don't work on me anymore."

"I'm not taunting you. I want you in here. Naked. I want to feel you against me again. It's all I can think about."

Nea's heart jerked in her chest. "Galath, you and me... *No.* I don't like you, and we infuriate each other. You keep secrets."

"If you want my secrets, I'll give them to you."

She stared at the dark look in his eye and fought back a shiver. She highly doubted a man like Kaden would ever share his soul with anyone.

He leaned closer, the water lapping around him. "Do you want me inside you again?"

His words sent a shot of heat arrowing through her body. Her pulse skittered.

"I can still feel how tight—"

"Be quiet." She shoved him. "You are—"

He grabbed her wrist. She teetered on the edge of the pool, then he yanked her forward.

Nea fell into the pool on top of him with a splash.

NEA CAME UP SPLUTTERING. "YOU *GUL*."

She shoved Kaden, her hands on his chest. A touch he liked far too much. Then she yanked her hands back, like touching him burned her.

Kaden smiled. Her hair was drenched, but she looked beautiful.

"Don't smile at me." She slapped her palm against the surface of the water, splashing him. "I swear you exist to vex me."

His gaze dropped. Her beige shirt had gone transparent, clinging to her skin. Her nipples were visible, and he swallowed a groan.

She splashed him again, and this time he splashed her back. Their gazes locked. She backed up a step and Kaden advanced.

Suddenly, there was another splash in the water nearby and they both tensed.

A small, sleek body covered in dark fur raised its head out of the water. Huge dark eyes blinked at them, then the creature twisted its body, slapped its tail, and splashed them.

"What the *gul*?" Nea raised an arm against the water.

Kaden's implant reeled off information. "I don't have a record of the creature, but it seems to be harmless." The animal bobbed around, moving past them in the water. It splashed them a few more times, before turning to look at them, an eager look in its eyes.

"It wants to...play," Nea said.

He splashed the animal, and it went into fits of

delight, thrashing around in the water. "Come on, Nea, play a little."

"I play."

"When?"

She scowled at him. "Okay, I'm too busy to play. I bet you never play."

"No, but sometimes I wish I did." The creature swam up to him and he stroked its sleek fur. It darted across to Nea, and she did the same. It turned onto its back, offering its lighter underbelly for a rub.

She laughed and complied. "I always wanted a pet, but my father wouldn't allow it."

Kaden cocked a brow. "I always got the impression your father would do anything for you."

She made a choked sound. "Hardly."

There was something in that sound that made him frown. "I get that your father is...demanding."

"Try an impossible-to-please snob."

Kaden raised his brows. "But not to you."

"Especially to me. I'm his daughter. I have to be perfect. I have to live up to the Laurier name." The animal bobbed up and looked at them, then it dived into the water and disappeared. "Bye, little guy." Then Nea stiffened. "Wait, what do you mean, not to me? You know he was a snob to other people?"

"It's nothing."

"Kaden." Her face changed. "My father was a snob to you." She sloshed through the water, and she'd obviously forgotten that her shirt was providing no cover, and lovingly hugging her breasts. "He said something to you."

"It doesn't matter."

She crossed her arms. "It does. Tell me."

Kaden sighed. "I don't care what your father thinks."

"What did he say?" Her tone said she wasn't giving up.

Looking out over the oasis, Kaden dragged in a breath. "He made it clear he believed that no-name trash like me should not sully the halls of the Academy." He heard her swift intake of breath. He looked back and met her gaze. "And that I was not to ever touch his daughter."

Her lips pressed into a flat line. "Is that why you—?"

Kaden lunged forward and grabbed her arms. "Why I fucked you?" He growled. "No. I did that because I've been fighting my desire for you my entire life. Because you're beautiful, smart, determined, and so damn gorgeous that I sometimes can't think of anything but you."

Her mouth dropped open and she just stared at him.

Lifting a hand, he stroked some strands of wet hair off her face. "You are so beautiful, Nea."

She frowned. "At the Academy, you said I was plain. A boring nerd."

"I lied. I often lied to you, and myself."

Her gaze locked on him. He saw the questions in her eyes, but they were secrets he couldn't share with her yet. He slowly pulled her closer.

"Galath, what are you doing?"

"Touching you." He pressed his lips to her jaw and felt her shiver. Her hands flexed on his chest.

"I told you this wasn't happening."

"I know, but you didn't mean it."

She made a sound. "You drive me crazy."

"You've been driving me crazy for years." He pressed his mouth to hers.

She pulled him close and kissed him back.

Nea moaned, pressing into him. She nipped his jaw, then kissed the hollow at the base of his throat. When she scraped her teeth over his skin, he growled.

He hauled her up and she wrapped her legs around his waist. She rubbed against him, her hot core pressed to his painfully hard cock. He slid his hands under her and cupped her tight ass.

She made a needy sound. He liked that she felt as much as him. She'd been tense, and he'd hated seeing her that way. He rocked her, and knew his cock was hitting her in just the right spot.

"Kaden—"

"I want to watch you come for me."

"No talking." She kissed him again, hard and wild.

This time, Kaden groaned. She turned him inside out. The touch of her, the taste of her, it reached inside him to the cold, dark places.

Right now, all he could see and feel was Nea. He wanted to give her pleasure.

In that moment, it was his only mission.

He whirled and carried her through the water. He set her on the edge of the pool, watching the sand stick to her damp skin.

He pulled her wet clothes off her, and threw them on the ground.

"Kaden—"

"Quiet." Then because he needed to, he turned her around.

She braced her hands on the edge, looking back over her shoulder, her face flushed.

He stroked his hand down her spine, tracing her tattoo. "I love this." He ran his finger over the Oronis roses and their thorns. "The last thing I expected from you."

"No one...knows," she murmured. "My father would be furious if he found out."

"I don't want to talk about your father right now." Kaden leaned down and kissed the markings. He ran his lips over them, and she bucked beneath him. "They're beautiful. The tattoo suits you, because like the Oronis roses, you're strong and tenacious."

She drew in a ragged breath. "I got it after graduation. Something just for me."

With a hungry sound, Kaden spun her and lifted her onto the edge of the pool. He stepped between her legs. The water lapped at him, and did nothing to cool the desire burning inside him. He pressed a kiss to her shoulder. Her skin was so soft, for such a tough woman.

His next kiss was to the underside of her breast. She sucked in a deep breath. He peppered kisses over her stomach, and pushed her legs apart.

"Nea." His voice was guttural. He stroked his fingers through her folds. "So soft and wet."

"No." She tensed. "We can't do this."

He saw panic in her eyes. His hand tightened on her thigh. "Yes, you can, but I will never force you to do anything."

She jerked against him, but she didn't pull away. Her chest heaved.

Their gazes met, then she suddenly lifted her hips.

He lowered his head and licked her.

She moaned, her hips bucking up. He teased, licked, and sucked.

"You taste sweet and spicy, Nea." He nipped her inner thigh.

"Curse you, Kaden." She wrapped her legs around his head, her body bowing.

He kept pleasuring her. He felt her hand sink into his hair, holding him in place.

He closed his lips on the small, swollen nub at the top of her sex and sucked.

She made a husky, inarticulate noise. She yanked on his hair. "I'm close, Kaden. I—"

"Come, Nea. I've got you."

She made another sound, then tensed up. With a sharp cry, she came, her body shuddering.

He rested his face on her thigh, holding her through it. The power inside him writhed, wanted to take her again, pin her beneath him.

Closing his eyes, he breathed her in and leashed that need.

Finally, her body went lax. He lifted his head. She looked at him, her face unreadable.

"I think you needed that," he said.

"Maybe." She sighed. "Don't think this means—"

"—you like me. I know."

Her gaze dropped. "Do you—?"

"No. I'll just swim a few more laps of the pool." In order to get some sort of control on his cock. And put a lock on his need. "This was just for you."

She watched him, her lips parted. She looked like she couldn't quite work him out.

He liked keeping Nea Laurier guessing.

"Then we'll get that speeder fixed." He pushed away, then dived under the water.

As Kaden started his laps, he felt her watching him.

CHAPTER NINE

Nea sat on a rock and watched Kaden work on the speeder. She'd rinsed off her clothes and redressed. Unsurprisingly, they'd dried quickly in the bright sunshine.

With a muttered curse, Kaden ripped something out of the speeder engine. His brow was creased, and he leaned in, using an auto-tool to place a repair patch on the engine.

She'd never been good with engines, but she remembered that he'd always been good at the Academy when it came to tinkering with anything mechanical.

She shifted a little, and felt the throbbing tenderness between her legs. A reminder of how he'd pleasured her on the edge of the pool. A tremor rippled through her.

Suddenly, Kaden yelped and yanked his hand back, shaking it.

"What happened?" She slid off the rock.

"Just scraped my knuckles on this gul-vexed piece of—"

She grabbed his hand and saw his torn knuckles. Blood welled. Pulling her scarf free, she used the edge to clean the scrape.

Kaden didn't make a sound. She looked up and saw his glittering gaze watching her.

"It's not often anyone tends my wounds," he said.

"No, I guess a knighthunter has to be self sufficient." She imagined him alone on a mission, patching up any injuries by himself. Her stomach tightened.

He shrugged. "I was used to it. I didn't have parents, or a family growing up."

He seemed to regret his words and clamped his mouth shut.

Nea cocked her head. "I know you grew up in a care home with Ashtin."

A brief nod.

"What happened to your parents?"

He glanced off into the distance, and for a second, she thought he wasn't going to tell her.

"I never had any. I have no memories of them. My earliest memories are fighting for scraps on the back-streets of Aravena." He made a face. "Not all parts of our shining capital city are clean and beautiful."

"I'm sorry."

He shrugged. "You have nothing to be sorry for. Besides, it's my past. Things improved once I was in the care home."

But he'd been all alone. With no family, no one to look after him, fighting for survival. Even the care homes couldn't provide a loving family.

Then he'd arrived at the Academy with something to prove.

He'd once said she'd reminded him that he was nothing. She understood that a little more now.

"I'm sorry for what my father said to you."

"You have nothing to be sorry for."

She held his ice-blue gaze. "You deserved to be at the Academy, the same as everyone else who passed the entrance tests. And you're the best knighthunter we have."

She gave his knuckles another gentle wipe. She knew his combat implant would heal it up quickly. Then without thinking, she lowered her head and pressed a kiss to his hand.

When she straightened, he was watching her with an unreadable look.

"Is the speeder ready?" she asked.

He nodded. "We should get moving."

Soon they were racing away from the oasis, heading toward the Gek'Dragar base. Nea's speeder couldn't quite go full speed, but it was operational.

She glanced sideways at Kaden, and in an instant, she was back at the oasis, his mouth and hands on her. A hot, pleasurable release ripping through her.

Gripping the speeder's handles, she let herself relive it. He'd wanted to pleasure her, take care of her.

She was seeing sides of Kaden Galath that she'd never imagined. A prickly feeling filled her belly. There was more to the man than she'd imagined.

A ridge of hills rose up ahead. She knew the base was on the other side. She needed to set aside her feelings for the confounding man beside her. Right now, she had to focus on the mission.

They made it to the bottom of the ridge and slowed. Nea swung off her speeder. The sun was heading toward the horizon, but it was still hot. Then she noticed something in the sky.

"Kaden, look."

He tipped his head back, brow furrowing. Bright colors danced in the sky—blue, green, and red. They moved and morphed at a frenzied pace.

"The ion storm." He swiveled to eye the top of the ridge, his hands on his hips and his face set. "Time for our armor."

She nodded and pulled her scarf off. With a thought, her armor activated, wrapping around her body. She watched him do the same until he was clad in his fitted, black armor.

They needed to stay quiet as they approached the base. She had no idea if the Gek'Dragar had proximity sensors. She hoped not. They started climbing up the hill, loose rocks shifting under their boots.

At the top, they crouched and peered down at the landscape below. She instantly spotted the old, rusted structure built into the side of a neighboring ridge. There was a flat area in front of it, once probably used as a landing area for the cargo ships that come in and out moving the berillo.

She studied the area, and the large, closed hangar doors leading into the base. There was no sign of anyone.

Her stomach clenched. What if they were wrong, and the knightqueen wasn't here?

"Far side of the structure. In the shadow of those large rocks."

At Kaden's murmur, she swiveled her head. She spotted a faint movement near some giant boulders. A Gek'Dragar soldier leaned against a large boulder, his muscular body clad in gray armor, only a shade darker than his scaly skin.

Her pulse leaped. They waited, minutes ticking by slowly. Another Gek'Dragar walked out of a smaller door leading into the base.

He was moving in an unhurried manner, a blaster weapon in his hand.

"Not many guards," Kaden said. "They're trying not to attract attention."

"We still don't know if the knightqueen and Sten are even here." Nea blew out a breath. "Maybe the Gek'Dragar are just keeping a few guards here on duty."

Kaden's gaze narrowed. "These guards are top-tier, Nea. They're holding the best weapons, they're relaxed, but not lazy. They're aware of their surroundings. They aren't young and untried, nor are they old and relegated to a base in the middle of nowhere for their final years."

He was right. "Okay, then we'll wait for a chance to get inside."

"That's risky."

"We have to take it," she said. "We need to rescue Carys and Sten."

Suddenly, a blare of sirens cut through the desert air. They both dropped lower.

The large hangar doors of the base slowly opened

and a Gek'Dragar ship moved out of the base on transport rails.

It stopped in front of the doors in the center of the staging area. Nea saw several Gek'Dragar walk out of the base, circling the ship. It was an older model shuttle, but the engines looked in good condition.

"That's the ship they're going to use to move them," she said.

"They can't leave the planet." Kaden looked up. Nea did too, and they both looked at the dancing energy filling the sky with lots of bright colors. It was even stronger now.

Kaden pressed a hand to the side of his head. "I'm accessing the weather reports for tonight that the *Helios* sent." He cursed. "There's a tiny window in the storms. It's small, but they could use it if they had the right pilot."

Her hands clenched. "We *can't* let them take her off-planet."

"Agreed."

Guttural voices echoed from down below. The breath caught in her lungs.

"Kaden."

"I see them."

Several guards exited the base. They crowded around two people.

Sten towered over the knightqueen. She stood straight, her chin lifted. Her platinum hair was loose around her shoulders, her face pale. Her dress was torn and dirty, but she looked no less a queen.

Sten seemed steady enough. He had a hand on the queen's arm and Nea could just see the glowing dura-band binding their wrists together. Even from a distance, Sten's rugged face looked pissed but alert.

The guards led them to one side of the ship.

"They're doing preflight checks," she said. "When's the window in the storms?"

"Thirty minutes."

They didn't have much time.

"We go in," she said. "We use the element of surprise."

His mouth flattened. "We don't know how many guards are down there, or what weapons they have—"

She gripped his forearm. "This is our chance, Kaden. We have to take it. For the knightqueen, for Oronis."

He held her gaze for a long moment, then nodded. "Okay. We'll ride in on the speeders, and take down as many Gek'Dragar as we can. Then we get Carys and Sten."

"And get away as fast as we can." She was well-aware it wasn't the best plan. "I bet you've had worse odds."

"I have." He reached down and touched her jaw. "Stay safe, Nea. If you get hurt, I'll be very angry."

She felt her heart thud hard in her chest. "I'm a knightmaster."

"I know, but I'm feeling rather territorial over that body of yours." He rose. "Let's go take down some Gek'-Dragar, and rescue our queen."

Nea stood as well. "You and me, Galath." Something she never thought she'd say.

He smiled. "You and me."

THE SPEEDER VIBRATED BENEATH HIM. Kaden glanced at Nea. She was in full armor with her visor down. She looked like the formidable knight that she was.

He nodded.

She nodded back.

He accelerated, and his speeder flew over the crest of the ridge and down the other side.

Nea's speeder revved, keeping pace beside him.

They hit the flat and sped up. They were halfway across when the Gek'Dragar saw them. Kaden pushed his engine for more speed. He saw the guards push Carys and Sten back behind them.

More guards stepped forward and lifted their weapons.

He sent a message through his implant.

Ready?

Ready.

They broke off, as laser fire filled the air. He zigzagged, and started forming energy on one hand.

He raised his palm and fired.

Several spikes of red energy hit the Gek'Dragar guards. A second later, blue balls of light joined his red ones. Nea was riding one-handed, firing as well.

Carys? Sten?

Kaden tried to contact the pair, but there was no response. Their comms were blocked somehow.

Kaden circled around and kept firing.

Three Gek'Dragar jogged forward. They threw their arms out, and their muscles bulged. The *var* hit them, making their muscles grow and morph. He watched them rise in height, spikes erupting on their tails.

He turned the speeder to the side and leaped off. He threw his hands forward, freeing several spikes of red energy.

Several Gek'Dragar staggered back. Two blue bolts of energy hit. He glanced over and saw Nea kneeling on her speeder, a wicked bow in her hand. She let off two more bolts.

They rained their attack down on the guards and sent them scattering.

Kaden caught a glimpse of some other Gek'Dragar shoving Carys and Sten aboard the ship.

Gul. They couldn't let that ship lift off.

He saw Sten was trying to fight back.

Kaden teleported in. For a brief moment, the world blurred, then sharpened. He re-appeared behind several Gek'Dragar guards. He formed his twin swords and attacked.

He whirled and slashed. With a roar, his foes spun.

But Kaden threw himself closer, and skewered one, then dropped and slashed at another's legs.

Hot blood spilled onto the sand.

Kaden!

Nea's voice echoed in his head.

He whirled. Ice slid into his veins.

Three large robots rolled out of the base.

Gek'Dragar soldiers leaped out of the robots' way. There was a loud, metallic whir, as the large balls stopped. Eight metal legs sprouted from each robot as they unfolded.

They looked vaguely like spiders and were topped with large cannons. Lights blinked on them.

He watched one cannon swivel toward Nea.

No.

She ran across the sand, sprinting fast.

The robot fired, laser streaking behind her. She dived and rolled.

Kaden leaped into the air, raising his swords above his head. He landed on the robot and sliced the cannon barrel off. Then he sank his second sword deep into the metal and twisted.

The robot sagged, the lights winking out.

He leaped off it and rolled. As he came up, he saw the ship's engine start.

Gul, no. He ground his teeth together.

Lasers whined again. The other two robots were going after Nea.

Kaden ran. He teleported and reappeared right behind her.

She jolted.

"Some warning, Galath," she bit out.

They spun, back-to-back, as the two remaining robots skittered closer from either direction.

Kaden raised his hands, red energy crackling over his palms. A large, red ball grew between them.

Nea was doing the same, blue light growing.

"Ready?" she asked.

"Now!"

They both tossed their energy balls. He watched his red energy hit the robot. The electricity crackled over it.

Kaden leaped forward, swinging his swords and cut into one leg.

The robot tilted and he smiled briefly. He ran around it, slicing into the other metal legs. He grunted, cutting through the strong metal.

The robot collapsed onto the sand, whirring madly. He strode forward and sank his sword into the top. Sparks flared.

Then he heard Nea cry out.

He spun, heart contracting.

Smoke was coming from her robot. She stood beside it, her hand clamped her shoulder. He saw blood oozing between her fingers.

A Gek'Dragar guard with a blaster stood close by.

He'd shot her. Kaden's mouth flattened. He threw his arm out, tossing a spike of energy at the guard. It impaled the alien's chest.

The Gek'Dragar staggered backward, his mouth opening. He collapsed.

Then Kaden watched the robot lift one leg and slam it into Nea. She flew through the air, fell, and rolled across the sand. The robot skittered after her and brought its leg down, pinning her to the ground.

No. *No.*

Its cannon swung, aiming toward her.

But what was worse was the robot was damaged. The metal shell was heating up, turning orange.

No. It was going to blow.

Kaden ran, then teleported. He re-appeared beside Nea and crouched at her side.

Her gaze met his.

He pressed a palm to her shoulder, then teleported her alone to her speeder.

Safe. She was safe.

In the distance, he watched her push herself up, swinging back to look at him.

The robot beside him was glowing hotter. *Gul.* There was nothing he could do. He pulled power around him, ready to teleport again.

Whack.

The robot's leg hit him, and he flew up, then hit the ground hard. He tasted sand in his mouth.

He groaned and rolled.

"Kaden, move!"

Nea's voice ripped across the comm line.

At that moment, the robot's metal body turned from yellow to white.

He tried to summon the energy to teleport.

Boom.

Everything exploded.

Something hit his head, and the world went black.

CHAPTER TEN

K aden woke with a quiet groan.

Everything hurt. He winced. It wasn't the first time he'd woken up hurt, with no idea what had happened, or where he was. It probably wouldn't be the last.

He shifted, and burning pain traveled up his side and arms. *Gul*, maybe he was getting too old for this. He probed the back of his head and felt a faint trace of swelling.

Then he heard a pretty tinkling, musical sound, and a warm breeze washed over him.

He opened his eyes all the way.

He was lying on a pallet of blankets, on the floor of a room carved from beige rock. A roughly hewn opening gave a view of the desert beyond, and the metallic wind-chimes hanging from the ceiling. It looked like the sun had just set, the horizon painted a brilliant orange. The energy of the ion storm painted the darkening sky.

He frowned. *Where was he?*

He forced himself to sit up. He was wearing a simple tunic top and loose pants, made from a coarse, brown fabric. He glanced down, and saw his arms were pink and tender. He lifted his shirt and spotted a healing wound on his stomach.

It all came back to him. Attacking the base, seeing the knightqueen, fighting the Gek'Dragar and their robots.

Gul.

The explosion was the last thing he remembered. His combat implants were working hard to heal his injuries.

Nea. Where was Nea?

He swung his legs to the side, biting back a groan from the surge of pain.

"You get up, and I'll put you back down."

Nea strode in from a tunnel that went deeper into the hillside.

He hesitated.

"A new Academy recruit could take you at the moment, Galath." She knelt and helped him lean back on the pillows.

Then she swiveled to the small stone table beside his bed and lit an old-fashioned oil lamp. Warm light filled the space.

He swallowed, his throat dry.

She eyed him. Her hair was loose, and she was wearing casual clothes similar to his. She poured a glass of water from a nearby jug, and held it up for him.

"You're okay?" he asked. She looked fine, but he had to know.

"I'm fine." She held the water up to his lips. The

liquid was cool against his throat. "I had a small laser burn on my shoulder, but it's healing."

He grabbed her wrist. "Knightqueen Carys? Sten?"

Nea sighed and set the glass down on the table. "The Gek'Dragar ship got away."

Frustration cut through him, and he looked away, biting off a vicious curse. He looked back at Nea. "Tell me what happened."

"You heroically teleported me out of range of that *gul*-vexed robot."

She sounded pissed, but there was no way he'd apologize for saving her life.

"Then the machine blew up, right on top of you." She shoved a hand through her hair. "You were mid-teleport. It was chaos. Chunks of burning metal everywhere. You teleported part of the way toward me. I tried to get to you." She looked down, her hands twisted together. "You were lying there, unconscious. I had no idea if you were alive." She dragged in a breath. "The Gek'Dragar ship took off and I couldn't stop it. I managed to contact the *Helios*, but there's no way for us to get through the ion storm tonight." Her gaze met his. "I pulled you out. You were badly burned. I had to take down a few Gek'Dragar guards to get us away."

Kaden glanced around the smooth walls carved into rock. "Where are we?"

"I loaded you onto my speeder." A muscle ticked in her jaw. "I had no idea if you'd make it. Your injuries were terrible, and your breathing was labored—" her voice cracked. "I knew it was too much for your combat implants to deal with."

He reached out and took her hand. And yet here he was. Alive and breathing just fine. "What happened next?"

"An old lady appeared, riding this strange desert beast. She didn't say much, just looked at you and made an annoyed noise, then said to follow her. That she would help you." Nea shrugged. "Since I had limited options—" she gave a harsh laugh "—and by limited, I mean none, I followed her."

Nea went silent.

Kaden squeezed her fingers. "Nea?"

Her gaze flicked up, churning with emotion. "I had no idea on that ride if you were dead or alive."

His heart hit his ribs. She'd been worried about him. He could count on one hand the number of times someone had worried about him. "I thought you wouldn't mind if I died."

She kept staring at him. "I guess things have changed, because now I do."

He shifted his hand to the back of her neck and pulled her down.

Their lips brushed. *This.* This was what he needed. The raw sensations ignited things that pushed out the last vestiges of his pain.

"*Nea,*" he breathed.

There was a scraping sound, then uneven footsteps. Nea pulled back, just as an old woman bustled in.

She was of medium height and build, although her loose robes made her seem rounder. Her graying hair was a tangled mess, and her skin was tanned and weathered.

Her eyes were bright green. She had a faded spot pattern on her skin.

She wasn't Solari. It was hard to tell what species she was.

"He's awake? Good. Good." The old lady carried a tray with a steaming bowl of something on it. "Told you, girly, he'd be fine." The woman set the tray down on a small table near the bed. "The girl was worried about you."

"You helped heal me?" he said.

The woman waved a hand. "I know a few tricks. And I had some uldrill."

Kaden raised a brow. Uldrill was a highly potent healing substance. It was rare and expensive. Who was this woman?

"Now you're better, but you need to eat and rest." The woman shot Nea a sharp look. "Both of you."

"Who are you?" Kaden asked.

"My name is Alara."

"You're not from Solari, Alara, are you?" Nea asked.

The woman shrugged and looked away. She had a nervous, twitchy disposition. Kaden had seen it before in heavily traumatized people.

"This is my home now. Make sure he eats that, then come and find me. I'll have a full dinner prepared, but he needs something so he can get upright." She bustled out with a flap of brown robes.

NEA WALKED THROUGH THE TUNNEL, staying close to Kaden. He was upright, and walking, which was a small miracle, considering how badly he'd been hurt. But his gait was unsteady, and he kept pressing a hand to the wall. Of course, he refused to lean on her or let her help him in any way. Typical man.

She still remembered how burned he'd been—his skin raw and bloody where his armor had been damaged. He'd been so still. Her stomach clenched, an oily taste in her mouth.

He's fine now, Nea.

She kept telling herself it was because of the mission. She needed him to help save the knightqueen.

But Nea knew she was lying to herself. And doing that had a way of always coming back to torment a person.

The tunnel opened into a larger area. Light filtered down from the carved roof overhead, while shadows danced in the corners. There was some equipment stacked up against the walls.

Kaden paused and looked around. "We're in an old mine."

Nea nodded. "It looks like Alara appropriated an abandoned mine. She's using the tunnels as her home."

Kaden grunted. "Sensible. There'd be power and water."

They traveled down another short tunnel, and Nea could hear Alara humming nearby and moving around. They were clearly getting close to her main living quarters.

They stepped into another open space, well-lit by

lights on the wall. There were mats on the stone floor, and a large window with an array of wind chimes that were silent at the moment. Through the opening lay a stark view of the night-darkened desert.

Their host stood at the far wall, where a natural bowl was carved into the stone. Water splashed into it as she washed up.

Nea caught a glimpse of delicate, black tattoos winding around the woman's wrists. Frowning, Nea tried to think why they looked so familiar.

The older woman turned. "Ah, come. Sit." She waved at the pillows on the floor, scattered around a low table which held plates of food.

Kaden had already eaten the soup, but the way he looked at the food, Nea figured he needed more. He'd need the energy to fuel his healing.

Nea hovered as he sat, which earned her an annoyed look. She ignored it. She'd preferred he didn't faceplant on the floor. He might not like admitting it, but he was weak right now.

She sat down and eyed the unfamiliar foods—meats and some sort of vegetables in rich sauces. It was all fragrant, with a hint of spices. Suddenly she was starving.

"Eat." Alara sat across from them.

They all filled their plates. Nea helped herself to some freshly baked flatbread.

"Thank you, Alara," Kaden said. "For the food. It smells delicious. And for taking us in."

Alara made a sound, then chewed and swallowed. "Smooth words and a pretty face." She looked at Nea. "A charmer, this one."

"He can be." Although he rarely turned the charm her way. And she knew it wasn't his normal temperament. He was just playing a part. "His job makes him good at saying what's required."

Alara nodded. "A spy."

"A knighthunter," Kaden countered. "And I meant the words."

"Good." Alara nodded. "You're welcome. Anyone who is the enemy of the Gek'Dragar is a friend of mine."

"You don't like them?" he said.

"No." Alara hunched her shoulders and pushed her plate away, even though there was still food on it. There was turmoil in her eyes before she hid it.

Sympathy struck at Nea.

"Does anybody like them?" Alara shook her head. "They take and pillage and torture and kill."

Nea's chest tightened. "You were their prisoner."

The woman was silent for a long time. "Yes. But I escaped, and I just want to be left alone."

"They abducted our queen," Kaden said.

Alara looked down. "Is she still alive?"

"Yes, we saw her at that Gek'Dragar base. They put her on another ship."

Alara kept staring at the table. "She'll be dead before long."

Kaden growled. "No, she won't. We're going to find her and rescue her."

"But not tonight." Alara rose, smoothing her robes. "You need to rest and finish healing."

"Alara, do you know where they might have taken our queen?" Nea asked carefully.

"No." The woman waved her hands and shook her head. "I'm old. I'm tired. I'm going to my quarters." She pointed downward. "I sleep down there. It's more secure. You two can take the quarters upstairs, now that he's well enough to brave the stairs." She made a harrumphing sound. "I hate the stairs. Hard on my knees." She left in a flurry of robes.

"Good night," Nea called after her.

Kaden finished eating. "She knows something."

"Maybe, but it's painful for her." Nea paused. "Did you see her tattoos?"

He nodded. "I think they're Akamian."

Akamian. Nea wracked her brain. A species whose planet had been destroyed by the Gek'Dragar.

"We'll talk to her in the morning." Nea rose and picked up some of the empty plates. The least she could do after Alara had cooked was clean up.

By the time Kaden stood, he looked far steadier and healthier than he had before. There was a little more color in his face.

They took the stairs upward, through several empty levels. The mines had clearly been extensive. Nea slowed on the stairs, and ran her hand over the rock wall. She saw thin veins of metallic ore glowing silver.

"Berillo," Kaden said. "Those veins are too small to be worth mining."

They reached the top. Carved arches offered a view of the desert. The dancing colors of the atmospheric energy lit up the night sky and washed the desert in pale light. It made it look almost magical. She saw some stars were appearing in the sky as well.

There was a sound, and she turned and saw Kaden lighting an old oil lamp. It added a warm glow to the space.

Fresh blankets were piled on a flat bed in the corner. There was a small, carved basin for water, and another room beyond that. She wandered closer, and saw a shower shaped into the rock wall in a sinuous curve.

"The miners clearly liked their comforts," she said.

"Go and shower, Nea. I'll go after you." He scraped a hand over his face.

"You're feeling all right?" she asked.

"Yes." He gave her a faint smile. "I'm not dying on you, yet."

She sniffed. Emotion she refused to acknowledge washed through her. "Good. I still need you. For the mission."

He nodded. "For the mission."

She spun and headed for the shower, but the lie didn't sit well with her.

CHAPTER ELEVEN

K aden finished drying off. The shower had felt good. It was nice to be clean.

Sometimes on an undercover mission, he could go days without having food or a shower, or sleeping in a bed. He was used to it, but he'd never love it.

It was a warm night, so he just pulled on the loose, brown trousers. He studied the healing skin on his arms from the burns. It was still pink, but healing fast. He'd been lucky. He had Nea to thank for saving him.

He strode out into the main room and stilled. She was lying on the pallet of blankets, a thin sheet over her.

She glanced his way and her gaze snagged on his bare chest. Luckily, she couldn't see his back. It wasn't so pretty. Thankfully, the glow from the lantern was low.

He strolled over. Sleeping beside her would be a special kind of torture. "I can make a second bed—"

"Just lie down, Kaden. You're healing and you need a good sleep." She shot another glance at his chest. "The burns have healed up well."

He sat on the edge of the pallet and nodded. "I feel fine. I've been hurt a lot worse than this."

She frowned. "Really?"

He shrugged. "You know missions can get dangerous, especially when you're in enemy space."

"What was the worst?"

His hand flexed. Flashes of a cell cut through his head. Blood. Screams. He deliberately blocked them. That was something he never revisited. "I got dumped in the desert on Mishon Prime." He'd been ditched there by enemy agents after they'd beaten him half to death. "I was far from any settlements, and had no water."

He'd had no shoes either. The sand had scoured his skin and burned his feet. He'd walked for days.

"You made it out."

"Obviously." He smiled. "You know I'm too tough to die."

That got him an eyeroll.

"I followed the desert animals. There were these small reptiles. They could find tiny amounts of water in the sand, and it was enough that I didn't die." He'd been in bad shape, though.

She cocked her head. "Mishon Prime..."

Gul. He tensed.

"We got important intel from a knighthunter from Mishon Prime. It saved my ship and a small convoy we were escorting from an ambush." Her gaze narrowed. "That was you."

He shrugged. "Maybe. There've been lots of missions and lots of intel I've passed along. And there are lots of knighthunters." He shifted to lie down.

She reached out and touched his back. And the raised ridges on it.

He went as stiff as a board, fighting the fiery feel of her touch.

"What is—?" She shifted closer, and he heard the frown in her voice.

"It's time to sleep," he said. "I'm tired."

He tried to move again, but she held tight. And Nea was strong and stubborn. He felt her move, kneeling behind him. Then he heard her sharp gasp.

Kaden gritted his teeth.

Her fingers moved over the old scars crisscrossing his skin.

"What happened?" Her voice was low and quiet.

He didn't say anything.

"Being stuck in the desert on Mishon Prime wasn't the worst you've been hurt, was it?"

He blew out a breath. "It happened a long time ago."

Her fingers tightened on his skin. "*Kaden.*"

He looked at his hands. "I got caught on a mission in the Prameda Sector. It was early on, I wasn't very experienced. Plus, I was cocky."

She made a sound. "You?"

"I got caught by the Kantos."

She pulled in a harsh intake of air. "I know they're not known for being gentle."

No. Gentle was not a word anyone would ever use for the insectoid aliens. Thankfully allies of the Oronis, the Eon Warriors, had defeated the Kantos.

"They tortured you," Nea said quietly.

A muscle in his jaw ticked.

"The Prameda Sector." Her tone was questioning, like she was thinking it over.

Kaden swallowed and stayed silent. He'd already given too much away.

"How long did they have you?" she asked.

"Seven days."

"Kaden." Her hand followed the line of a scar.

"My injuries had healed by the time I was rescued. I could've had surgery to erase the scars…"

"But of course you wouldn't do that."

He felt a brush on his skin between his shoulder blades and he jolted. It was her lips. She pressed kisses to his back, tracing the old scars.

"Nea…"

"Quiet. I'm feeling soft toward you right now, and if you talk, you'll ruin it." More featherlight kisses. "I'm sorry you went through this."

He closed his eyes and just let himself feel.

"I'm sorry they hurt you. That you were alone."

Gul. His heart knocked against his chest.

"Now lie down." Her tone turned no-nonsense. "We both need some sleep. Tomorrow, we need to get back to the *Helios* and find the knightqueen." She moved and laid down beside him.

As Kaden settled on the pillows, she turned off the lantern. Shadows danced on the rock ceiling. He shifted, trying to relax.

But his mind was churning with the fact he'd shared his worst, most terrifying moment with Nea. Plus she was lying right there beside him.

He felt her push up on an elbow. "What's wrong?"

He didn't say anything.

"Galath, seriously. What's the problem? You must be exhausted."

Well, he wasn't going to tell her that his cock was half hard from just being near her, smelling her. "I'm not used to sleeping with someone beside me."

"Oh?"

"I've...never slept beside someone." It required far too much trust, something he didn't have in large supply.

"Ever?"

"Ever." He rolled on his side, away from her. "Don't worry. I'll fall asleep eventually."

"Well, I might not like you...much. But I won't kill you in your sleep."

He laughed. "I know that."

"You need to relax."

"I don't relax." Relaxing got you killed.

She made a humming sound. Then he felt heat at his back as she fitted her body to his.

Gul. His cock went hard.

"You need to stay still, because I don't want you to aggravate those healing burns." A slim hand slipped over his side to his chest, and sensations flared all over his skin.

His gut hardened. "Nea."

"Quiet."

Her fingers moved down, over his bare stomach, and he sucked in a breath. Then she pushed the waistband of his trousers down.

Kaden ground his teeth together. Her hand gripped his cock.

A groan escaped him. He felt her hot breath on the

back of his neck. Her fingers ran over the tip of his cock, which was already leaking for her.

Desire, hotter and bigger than anything he'd ever felt, seared through him.

He was at her mercy.

She started stroking him.

His muscles wound tighter. It was Nea's hand on his cock, Nea touching him. He felt the scrape of her teeth on his neck.

"So hot, so hard," she murmured.

He let out a low groan. His cock swelled and he knew he wouldn't last much longer.

"Let go," she whispered.

He obeyed. His body bowed, and he thrust his cock desperately into her palm. All his senses were filled with Nea.

Kaden came, his release spurting on his gut and her hand.

Afterward, he felt drained. There was no tension in him at all.

She slipped out of the bed and was back in a moment with a towel. She wiped his stomach, then settled his trousers back into place.

She pressed a light kiss to his neck. "Don't think this means—"

He choked out a laugh. "I know."

"Sleep now." Surprisingly, his eyelids lowered, and sleep dragged him under.

THE NEXT MORNING, Nea checked the speeder, prepping to leave. She'd left Kaden sleeping, figuring he needed it.

She'd woken up plastered against him, with her head on one muscled bicep and an arm and leg thrown possessively over him.

She shook her head. The morning sunshine was already hot on her skin. Having some fresh air helped clear her head. Sort of.

Sharing a bed with Kaden had been...enjoyable. Too enjoyable.

He was a knighthunter. A dangerous one. Playing house with him wasn't something she should get used to.

Inside, Alara was humming in the living area, and the smell of cooking food filled the air. The older woman was making them breakfast.

Nea had remembered a little about the Akamians and those tattoos. Her stomach hardened. She needed to ask Alara some questions.

Focusing on the speeder again, she checked Kaden's repair patch was still holding. The vehicle was parked under an overhanging rock. It would carry both of them back to where they'd hidden the shuttle.

She glanced up and wondered if Kaden was awake.

Memories hit her. The feel of him, stroking his long cock, giving him pleasure. She stopped, closed her eyes, and shivered.

She'd enjoyed it. She'd wanted to...take care of him.

She opened her eyes, and stared sightlessly at the desert awash in bright sunshine. Seeing the evidence of his torture...it had hurt her to see that. She could imagine him alone, in pain, scared, knowing that no one was coming for him.

She knew he'd been hurt in the desert on Mishon Prime, getting intel that had helped her. And she knew in her gut that he'd gotten those scars while getting information that had saved her life.

She bit her lip. He'd been tortured by the Kantos in the Prameda Sector. There had been other missions where she'd received intel just in time. But she remembered intel from a knighthunter from the Prameda Sector had saved her life. She'd almost walked into an ambush. That intel had ensured her mission success, and she'd received a commendation.

All thanks to intel from a nameless knighthunter.

In fact, she remembered now that the Knightforce commanders had complained that a knighthunter had gone off the plan in order to get it, and had been reprimanded.

She pressed a hand to her stomach. How many of her missions had succeeded because Knighthunter Kaden Galath had risked his life?

And why?

He'd never liked her. He'd made that clear...or had he? He was good at only showing what he wanted people to see. Gul, the man had more confusing pieces than a game of master beraja.

"Morning."

His deep voice made her turn.

He stood there in his armor, angular face handsome and aloof. Every inch the knighthunter.

"Good morning," she said. "Feeling all right?"

"I feel great. The best sleep I've ever had."

She thought there was a faint flush in his cheeks. "Good."

"Nea." His gaze was on her lips as he stepped closer.

Yes, kiss me. She knew it was crazy, but she wanted it. Needed it.

They both stepped toward each other.

"Breakfast." Alara appeared in the rock archway, wiping her hands on a towel. "Eat it now while it's hot."

Nea saw annoyance flash on Kaden's face, until he smoothed his features out and turned. "Thank you, Alara."

The woman snorted. "You can kiss the girl later." She disappeared inside.

A laugh broke out of Nea. She saw Kaden's mouth twitch, then he waved at the doorway.

Soon they were seated on the pillows at Alara's table, eating the delicious food. There was more fresh bread, eggs of a desert lizard, and some small, succulent fruit.

"You'll go after your queen," Alara said.

Kaden nodded. "We never give up."

"Not until we find her and bring her home," Nea added. "Although, we've lost the ship they took her on. We don't have a lot to go on."

Alara toyed with her food, seemingly lost in thought. Nea didn't want to dredge up bad memories for the woman, but they couldn't abandon Carys and Sten.

"We appreciate all your help." Nea met Kaden's gaze, and he nodded. Nea swallowed. "Alara, do you know where the Gek'Dragar might take our queen?"

"No. *No.* I wouldn't know." She shook her head.

"You were their prisoner once." Nea paused. "I saw the tattoos on your wrist when you were washing up."

Alara yanked the sleeve of her shirt down.

"They're royal tattoos of the Akamians," Nea said.

"The Akamians are no more." Alara fiddled with her fork. "Destroyed."

"By the Gek'Dragar," Kaden said quietly. "The Royal family were taken and killed...but you escaped."

Alara lifted her head, and horrors danced in her eyes. "The past is the past. I'm Alara of the desert."

"But once, you were something else," Nea said softly. "And the Gek'Dragar took you somewhere. A prison. That's likely where they took our queen, isn't it?"

Alara stood, and bumped into the table. The plates rattled.

Nea rose as well and held out her hand. "I don't want to upset you, or force you to revisit old hurts."

Alara stood as still as a statue.

"But *please* help us. You could help our queen and her knightguard live. It would be a small bit of justice against the Gek'Dragar."

"I couldn't save my family," Alara whispered.

"I'm so sorry for that," Nea said. "But you can help save Knightqueen Carys and her guard, Thorsten."

The older woman bit her lip so hard that it had to hurt.

Nea took Alara's hand. Her skin was thin and wrinkled, her fingers were cold. "Please?"

Alara gripped Nea's hand. Her grip was firm.

"Ti-Lore. The prison is on Ti-Lore. It's a cliff world. A mining planet a bit like Solari, but different." Her brow creased. "They never let me out." Her face fell. "There were so many screams in that rocky prison."

Nea's heart hurt for her. "Where is Ti-Lore, Alara?"

The woman swallowed. "I don't know. I was transported there and out without ever knowing. I'm sorry."

Nea nodded and smiled. "It's a start, one we desperately needed."

Kaden nodded, as well. "It helps. A lot. Thank you."

Alara pained gaze met theirs. "I hope you find your queen, before they destroy her."

CHAPTER TWELVE

B ack aboard the *Helios*, Kaden paced the bridge, listening to Chief Engineer Watson.

"The ship that left Solari isn't travelling under cloak. So we can't track a camouflage trail. We can follow the engine trail, but it's not as reliable."

Captain Attaway frowned. "We could lose it. It's already got a head start."

"We think we know where they're taking the knightqueen," Nea said.

She was back in her regular, fitted black suit. There was no sign of the relaxed woman with her hair loose who had shared a bed with him.

"We were helped by a woman on Solari," Nea continued.

"She saved my life," Kaden told them.

Nea nodded. "Her species, the Akamians, were wiped out by the Gek'Dragar."

"That's terrible," the captain said.

Kaden crossed his arms. "She was royalty, and she was the Gek'Dragar's prisoner."

The captain sucked in a breath, crossing her hands behind her back. "And this woman knows the location of the Gek'Dragar's maximum-security prison?"

Kaden nodded. "It's on a cliff world called Ti-Lore."

"Where is it?" the captain said. "We'll plot a course."

"That's the problem," Kaden said. "We don't know. I've never heard of it, and we have no idea where it is."

"If we've never even heard a whisper about it, it's likely no one has." Nea put her hands on her hips and frowned.

Kaden felt waves of frustration coming off her. He wrestled with the idea forming in his head. He didn't like it. He didn't want to take Nea there.

"Kaden?"

He looked up and saw her watching him.

"You thought of something," she said.

Gul. She read him so easily. "I know someone who might be able to help. If anyone knows where Ti-Lore is, it's him."

"Who?" she said.

"His name is Hager."

Nea's mouth tightened. "And?"

Kaden raked a hand through his hair. "He's a former Ktin navigator."

Nea blinked. "Former?"

"He left the Ktin military."

"No one leaves the Ktin." Nea frowned. "They don't let their people leave, especially their navigators."

"Who are the Ktin?" Captain Attaway asked.

"A militaristic species," Nea said. "They stay clear of the Oronis, so we have no trouble with them. Their navigators are...plugged into their ships. Their ships are semi-organic, and the navigators are given huge quantities of a drug called *jarra* to facilitate the link. They initiate interstellar jumps, navigate across star systems, have a near-perfect recall of everywhere they travel." She looked at Kaden. "They usually burn out very young."

"And lose their minds," he said. "Well, Hager knew it was coming and left. He hides on the planet Prozula."

Nea groaned. "You're joking."

"No."

"Nea?" the captain prodded, clearly disliking being in the dark.

"Prozula is a planet in a small pocket of space that nobody claims," Nea said. "The planet has several moons, and is surrounded by lots of space junk. It's home to pirates, smugglers, thieves, and thugs."

"It sounds lovely," the captain said dryly.

"Prozula is a rough world known for—"

"—its illegal fight rings," Kaden said. "It has cage fights, clubs, games. You name the style of fight, and you'll find it there."

"And people betting on it," Nea said.

"Yes," he confirmed. "The bloodier the fights, the more spectators they get. The worst of them are to the death."

"Jesus," Chief Watson muttered.

"Hager runs one of the most successful fight clubs," Kaden said. "It's called Slam."

"You've been there?" Nea asked.

He shrugged. "Once or twice. Look. Let me go to Prozula and talk to Hager. Alone."

Nea straightened. "No way, Galath. This is *our* mission. I'm coming."

He felt a muscle in his jaw clench.

"Hager isn't fond of strangers."

"I don't care. Captain, set a course for Prozula," Nea ordered. "The location is in the star map database."

Captain Attaway gave one last glance at Kaden. "You got it, Knightmaster."

Kaden grabbed Nea's arm and lowered his voice to a lethal rasp. "Prozula is no place for you."

Her chin lifted. "Because I'm too good? Too proper?"

"Yes." She didn't need to see the filth. The worst of the worst.

"I'm no princess, Kaden."

He sighed. "I'm just trying to protect you."

"And I'm just trying to protect you." She pulled away and strode over to talk to the captain.

Protect him? His mind couldn't make that work. Kaden blew out a breath. It looked like he was taking Nea to Prozula.

Gul.

Several hours later, he stood, staring out at the viewscreen as Prozula grew larger with their approach.

It was a small, dark sphere, whose blackness was broken only by glowing lights. There were no farmlands, or green, open spaces. Space junk filled the orbit around it. They'd already diverted course numerous times to avoid some larger pieces of junk.

He heard the whisper of the bridge doors behind him, and sensed Nea coming.

"Well? Will I blend?"

He turned. She wore slick black-leather pants that hugged her hips, with a wide belt at her narrow waist. She had a red tank top that clung to her torso, and a short, beaten-up, brown jacket. The tank displayed a strip of bare skin around her middle. His hand clenched. Her dark hair was up in a ponytail.

She'd cause a riot. She was gorgeous, and clearly competent, and every male on Prozula would be fighting not to get hard.

He sniffed. "You'll do."

Her gaze ran down his body then back up. "You look disreputable."

His brown leather trousers were tucked into black boots. His tight shirt was blue-gray, and he had a knife strapped to one thigh.

"It's better if I go alone," he tried again. "Hager hides in plain sight, but he's cautious. He only deals with people he knows personally."

"You'll vouch for me."

"Nea, Hager isn't nice."

"I know, Kaden." She arched a brow. "I can deal with people like Hager."

He sighed. "Fine. Captain, it's safer if you keep the *Helios* in high orbit around the planet to avoid the worst of the junk. We'll teleport down. Any shuttle that lands on Prozula will be stripped for parts in under twenty minutes."

Nea nodded. "Let's do this."

THEY TELEPORTED INTO A DARK, narrow alley. Music thumped nearby, and raucous shouts punctuated the night.

For a second, Nea's head swam as she adjusted after the disorientation of the teleport. Strong hands gripped her biceps.

"Steady?" he asked.

"I'm good." After the teleport, Kaden, of course, looked fine.

Teleportation was such a rare ability. She still got the feeling that there was more to Kaden and his powers than he let on.

"Club Slam is close by. Stay close. Hager's customers are not known for their manners."

"And you know I can handle myself."

He shot her a faint smile. "I do."

Shadows moved deeper in the alley, and she tensed, ready for anything. But Kaden didn't seem worried. He towed her toward the mouth of the alley. The paved street beyond was filthy, and lined with clubs.

"All of them offer fights?" she asked.

"Yes. And plenty of other vices." He strode down the sidewalk with a powerful stride.

Several people got out of his way. A few women dressed in tiny wisps of fabric watched him with hungry interest.

Nea glared at them as she walked past until they looked away.

It was stupid. He wasn't hers. She...hated him.

Although the word seemed wrong now. More like a shoe that no longer fit right.

Kaden headed toward a large building, topped with a dome. Lights strobed from inside it. Outside, there was a long line to get in.

He bypassed the line, striding straight toward the guards at the front door. They were four huge Scollins. A species known for their brawn and aggressiveness. They were as broad as they were tall, with bald heads and heavy brows.

One scowled at Kaden, then his brow lifted. "Kai. It's been a long time. Welcome back."

Kaden lifted his chin.

Kai?

The guard eyed Nea. "You brought a friend for once." He gave Nea a long, lazy look.

"Careful," Kaden warned. "She hits."

"Hard," Nea added.

The guard smiled, then stepped back and waved at the door. "You're in the right place, then."

Kaden pressed a hand to the small of her back and ushered her into Club Slam.

The interior was dark, with the exception of bright strobes of blue light passing over the space. Patrons were packed into the space, shoulder to shoulder. Nea picked up the scents of perfume, sweat, and adrenaline.

Kaden took her hand, and she didn't fight it. He knew this place, not her.

"Kai?" she said.

"An alias I use. In some places, it's best not to announce that you're a knighthunter."

They reached the center of the space, the room becoming larger, the dome arching overhead. Now, she could hear grunts, and the rhythmic sound of flesh hitting flesh.

Someone screamed, and the crowd cheered.

Her mouth tightened. *Nice.*

Ahead, a huge cage dominated the center of the club. Two people were inside, fighting with heavy, vicious hits.

There were smaller, open rings dotted around. Spectators clustered around each fight, cheering, booing, and laughing. Long bars lined the sides of the room, lit up with blue lights. A quick glance showed her that they were selling everything: drinks, various drugs, scantily clad men and women.

She forced herself to keep her face blank.

"I can feel your disgust," Kaden said.

She shrugged. "Let's find your friend and get the information we need."

They moved closer to the central cage. As they neared, she saw the fighters clearly now. One was a huge Inketh, who was shirtless, his bulky muscles gleaming with sweat. His face was twisted with focus and fury. Inketh used rage to amp up their body's natural fighting instinct. They were dangerous fighters, and often mercenary soldiers.

His competitor was smaller, some sort of humanoid, who didn't look like there was any fat on him. His face was bruised, but he bounced on his feet, vibrating with energy.

The pair clashed again. The smaller fighter was fast, and he used it to his advantage, slamming a flurry of punches into the Inketh's abdomen. The Inketh growled and shoved his competitor away. They clashed again, jabbing and swinging at each other. As fists connected, Nea looked away.

"Not your sort of entertainment?"

She glanced at Kaden. "I don't mind watching a fight." She glanced up at the cage as the bigger alien rammed the smaller one against the mesh side. "But I like rules."

"Of course, you do." There was an amused smirk on his face.

"I like to see two well-trained, well-matched opponents test each other. Not this blood sport."

"You and I agree on something again." He looked over her shoulder and his smirk dissolved. "There's Hager."

Nea followed the direction of his gaze.

The Ktin lounged on a huge, throne-like chair near the cage. It sat a little higher than the crowd, giving him a perfect view of the fight and the club. He was watching the fight, a glass of some red fluid cradled in his hand. Several women hovered nearby, trying to capture his attention.

Nea could see why. He was handsome, in a dark, dangerous way. His black hair was long, and fell well past his shoulders. His face was rugged, and it looked like his nose had been broken before and hadn't healed correctly. The imperfection just added to his appeal. His body looked fit and muscled.

Kaden pulled her closer.

Hager spotted them, his gaze sharpening. He raised a dark brow.

Kaden stopped at the base of Hager's chair. "Hager."

"Kai. It's been a while." The man's gaze moved to Nea. "Who's this?"

"Nea. She's mine."

She tried not to bristle at the pronouncement, but she did shoot Kaden a look.

Hager chuckled. "I'm not sure she knows that."

"She knows," Kaden said.

"What brings you to my sinful little part of the galaxy?"

"I need some intel."

"Mmm."

"You know I always make it worth your while."

"You do."

In the cage, the Inketh downed the humanoid, who lay face first on the stained floor, groaning. The Inketh lifted his massive fists and roared at the crowd.

They chanted his name.

As Kaden talked with Hager, Nea looked around. The place was packed. Then she spotted some familiar forms and froze. *Gek'Dragar.*

But as she watched, she noted the pair were relaxed, watching a fight in one of the rings. Then one raised his head and looked her way. His green eyes gleamed in the dim light.

He didn't show any recognition before his gaze moved back to the fight.

Suddenly, a hand slid down her arm.

"Beautiful. I want you, female."

She looked to the side. A male of an alien species she didn't recognize was smiling at her. He was huge, with bulging muscles, and no discernible neck. He had a wide face, with dark, swirling markings across his cheeks. His skin was a deep-amber color, with a slightly bumpy texture.

"One, I have a name," Nea said. "And two, I don't care what you want."

"Your skin is so smooth."

He rubbed his fingers across her wrist.

Ugh. She was getting mad, and the last thing she needed was to cause a scene. "Look—"

Suddenly, she was jerked back against a hard body.

"Don't touch her."

The hairs on the back of her neck rose. Kaden's voice was a dark growl. She looked up, and saw his face was hard, a little scary.

"I want her," the alien said. "I am Koor, and I take what I want."

"Not tonight." In a lightning-fast move, Kaden slammed his hand against the man's throat. The alien gagged and doubled over.

Kaden glared at the man.

Koor rose, rubbing his neck. Then he roared. "I demand you fight me! I will win the female."

Nea raised her brows. "Really?"

"You couldn't handle her," Kaden said.

Hager stepped into view. "The challenge has been issued, Kai. You have to fight." He stepped closer and lowered his voice. "If you win, I'll give you the intel you're after."

CHAPTER THIRTEEN

"This is a bad idea." Nea paced the small prep room. Hager had given it to Kaden so he could get ready for the fight.

It had bare, concrete walls, a few lockers, and a scarred table. The dull thud of music came through the thin walls.

Kaden was wrapping his hands with tape.

"It will be fine, Nea."

"The guy is huge," she said.

He looked over. "You don't think I can win?"

She thrust her hands on her hips. "I know you can win, but you'll still take a few hits."

He shrugged, and annoyance jabbed at her. *Men.*

"It'll be worth it," he said.

"So we can get the intel on Ti-Lore."

His smile was sharp. "No. Because that *gul* touched you."

Her belly was suddenly alive with flutters. He was doing this for her?

Kaden flexed his hands, and stripped his shirt off. His pale skin gleamed, highlighting the lean strength of his musculature.

She swallowed, and the flutters in her belly moved lower.

He stalked toward her. She smelled his dark, spicy scent, sensed his readiness for the fight.

"Do I get a kiss for good luck?"

"I don't think you need it."

His head lowered, his mouth hovered over hers. "What if I want it?"

By the stars above, he twisted her up. She rose up on her toes, and pressed a quick kiss to his tempting lips. "Let's get this over with."

"As you command, Knightmaster."

She stared at him, then opened the door. Music, the jeers of the crowd, and the sound of fighting assailed them.

Kaden slung an arm across her shoulders, pulling her close. She tried to move, but he held her tight.

They headed toward the cage. Hager saw them coming and smiled.

"It's been too long since you've been in the cage, Kai."

Nea controlled her jerk. *He'd fought here before?*

"Let's get started." Kaden looked at Nea. "Stay right here. Don't wander off."

"Just get it done." She paused, then grabbed his arm. "And don't get hurt."

He winked at her, then whirled to face the cage.

One of the guards opened the cage door for him.

Koor was already in the center of the cage, working up the crowd.

When Kaden entered, the spectators went wild. A lump lodged in her throat.

"Don't worry, Kai's girl," Hager said. "He's good."

"I know that. It doesn't mean I like this."

"Feisty. I see why he likes you."

Nea shifted closer to the mesh. Her pulse was drumming. The announcer was shouting in some alien language that her inbuilt translator didn't know. A gong sounded.

Kaden looked cool, calm, and bored.

Koor roared and raced at him with rage and energy.

Kaden sidestepped, then landed a hard hit to Koor's side.

The crowd went wild.

The fight had begun.

Kaden was faster. She watched him weave and whirl. He ducked hits, his body fluid and athletic. He landed several hard blows. This was no elegant Oronis fight. This was hard, dirty, and brutal.

Koor caught Kaden with a punch to the gut. Nea winced, and Kaden grunted and fell back a step.

"I'll take your woman," Koor bellowed. "When I'm done, she won't remember your name, let alone your cock."

Nea rolled her eyes.

Kaden didn't get riled, instead, he stilled. Like a lethal predator spotting prey ready for the kill.

She gripped the mesh.

Kaden launched forward.

In that moment, Nea realized he'd been merely playing with Koor before. *Now* he was fighting.

With his face set like stone, Kaden hammered kicks and punches into Koor. Kaden's opponent tried to fight back, but he was slowing down and clearly hurting. Blood splattered the floor of the cage.

Koor let out another roar. He got in a lucky hit and caught Kaden's jaw.

She saw Kaden grit his teeth. His eyes glittered.

His next round of punches was brutal, unrelenting, and powerful. Perspiration covered Kaden's chest. Her pulse fluttered and she pressed her thighs together. Violence had never turned her on, but a good fight and excellent skills did.

Kaden was amazing.

The next blow sent Koor to his knees.

Kaden looked over the man's bowed head, and his gaze collided with Nea's. It was hot and hungry.

Her lips parted and she gripped the mesh harder. Koor struggled to get up, but Kaden's next kick sent him to the floor, moaning.

"We have a winner," the announcer cried. "Kai!"

The crowd erupted in cheers and undulating cries.

Nea's pulse was pounding, raw desire hot in her blood. She watched Kaden stride to the door of the cage, unwrapping his hands.

People slapped his back as he tossed the wrappings to the floor.

Nea couldn't move, she just kept staring. Kaden stared back at her, then headed her way.

The crowd parted.

"Kai, well done," Hager called.

"We'll talk in a minute." Kaden's voice was low, edgy. He grabbed Nea's hand, then pulled her through the crowd.

———

BLOOD POUNDED through Kaden's system, both from the fight and from Nea watching him. His chest felt heavy, his gut was heavy, and need was thick and hot in his blood.

He saw the guard by the door to the prep room they'd used before. Kaden jerked his head. The guard nodded and opened the door.

"Kaden—" Nea began.

He pulled her inside and kicked the door closed behind them. He spun her and pushed her against the wall, his hands on either side of her head.

He saw her lick her lips.

Gul, he felt that in his cock. "You liked watching me fight."

"You fight well."

He ran his nose along hers, breathing her in. "I fought for you."

She pressed her hands to his chest. "I know."

He heard the desire in her voice. There was nothing inside him at that moment except his need for her.

Desire. Want. Other things he didn't have names for.

She grabbed his face, and turned his head. Their mouths met.

He thrust his tongue into her mouth. He opened her

lips wider, kissing her deeply. Finally, *finally* he tasted her again. The unique flavor that was all Nea.

She made a husky sound, her fingers digging into his chest. Her tongue stroked his. She didn't seem to care that he was covered in sweat and smeared with his opponent's blood.

"Nea." His voice was a deep rasp. "You taste good, feel good."

"No talking," she breathed.

"This time, I want to talk." But he also needed more. He needed her. He quickly unfastened her trousers and shoved them down. "Take them off, Nea."

She kicked them away, her chest heaving.

Kaden's cock was throbbing, need hurtling through him. Then he urged her up and she wrapped her legs around his hips. He ground her against the wall, pinning her with his body. He kissed her again, thrusting against her. His hands clenched on her ass.

She cried out, then rubbed against him. His cock pressed against her stomach.

Kaden shoved the waistband of his trousers down and his cock sprung free. "Hold on tight," he warned her.

Her eyes flashed. "I can take whatever you give me, Galath."

"Kaden. Say my name."

"*Kaden.*" She sounded like a queen commanding her knight.

He tilted her hips, then slammed home.

Nea cried out, her body clamping down on his.

So good. So perfect. He thrust into her again and again. He felt her short nails score his back.

"*Here,*" he murmured hotly. "Right here is where I belong."

"Faster," she panted. "Harder."

"You'll take me. However I give it, you'll take it."

She bit his ear. "Stop talking."

He stepped back, carrying her, keeping his cock lodged inside her. Two steps and they reached the table. He set her on it. *Gul,* she was gorgeous.

He pulled out, and thrust back into her. Every cry she made drove him higher. Every pleasure center in his body was on fire.

He pushed her knees back, the table rocking beneath them. She took every thrust, moaning, gripping him hard.

He moved a hand between them and found that swollen nub.

She arched. "*Oh...* I'm close."

"I want to feel you come," he growled.

With the next stroke of his thumb, she exploded. He watched her come, and slid his hand up and around her neck, feeling her wild pulse. Her inner muscles clamped down hard on his cock, but he gritted his teeth and held off his own release. He wasn't done yet.

Kaden felt savage. Driven by the need to claim her. He kept thrusting inside her, his gaze locked on hers.

"*Yes.* Take me, Kaden." Her fingers clamped on his wrists.

"No one's fucked you like this before."

"*No one.*"

He changed the angle of his thrusts. "I want you to come again."

"Kaden—"

He grunted as he surged inside her. "Come again."

"I—" Suddenly, she came again, crying out his name. She arched under him, taking all of him.

On the next thrust, his orgasm ripped through him.

His back snapped upright, and he threw his head back and groaned through the deluge of pleasure.

He dropped forward, and pressed his face to her hair. He heard the rasp of their breathing. Felt her fingers flex on his slick skin.

"Kaden—"

"Shh, Nea. Just... For now, just feel."

She didn't respond, but her hands roamed up his back. When the thump of loud music intruded, reality did, too. Reluctantly, Kaden straightened and pulled out of her.

She bit her lip.

"Okay?" He stroked her jaw.

She smiled. She looked so debauched, but she didn't seem to care.

"Yes." She sat up. "Luckily my father can't see me."

The words were like ice cold water spilling over Kaden. Oh, yes, if her father knew Kaden had his dirty hands on his precious daughter, he wouldn't be happy. Kaden yanked his trousers back into place.

"Right." It felt like a rock had lodged in his chest. "The great Torquin Laurier would hate seeing his princess fucked by no-name trash like me."

Nea stilled and her brow furrowed. "That's not what—"

Kaden turned away. "Clean up. We need to talk to Hager and find out where Ti-Lore is."

His gut churned with a stew of feelings and emotions, and he couldn't quite get a grip on them. He yanked his shirt over his head. "You forgot to add your usual line. That I shouldn't think this means you like me."

Her frown deepened. "Kaden, wait, I—"

"Don't worry, I won't forget. I'll wait outside." He slammed out of the room.

The noise of Slam hit him. He dragged in a breath and bit back a curse. He already knew he'd overreacted, but old hurts were digging their claws in.

The guard at the door smirked at him. He'd probably heard them. Kaden just scowled and ran a hand through his hair.

His mission was what he needed to focus on right now. He needed to get his head on straight.

CHAPTER FOURTEEN

Nea finished fastening her trousers and belt. She ran her hand through her hair. Her hair tie was long gone.

And she was pretty sure she looked like she'd just been well fucked. She was sticky between her legs and sensitive. Kaden hadn't been gentle.

And she'd loved every second.

Well, until the end, where he'd stalked out on her.

She pressed a hand to her unsteady stomach. She wasn't exactly sure what was going on in his head. He was usually so controlled. Yes, he broke the rules, and took some reckless risks, but she was certain he thought them all through before he did.

This outburst wasn't like him.

She shook her head. She couldn't worry about it right now when they were stuck on Prozula. They needed the intel on how to find Ti-Lore. Then, they needed to get out of there.

She strode out the door and spotted Kaden nearby, his tense back toward her.

"Let's talk to Hager." She strode past him.

The music and the sound of the fighting sounded loud and harsh now.

"Nea—"

He sounded contrite, but she didn't look at him. "Like you said, we need to focus on the mission."

She strode back through the crowd toward Hager, who was still holding court next to the fight cage.

People yelled congratulations to Kaden and slapped his back. Women sidled up to him. Nea kept her focus on Hager.

The man had a small smirk on his face as he studied them.

"Kai, a magnificent fight as always."

Kaden grunted. "Time to talk."

Hager nodded and glanced at the fighters in the cage. "I'm not missing anything here, anyway."

Nea glanced over and saw the fighters were unskilled and sloppy.

Hager rose. "Come."

They followed him to a door at the back of the club. Two huge guards opened the door for them as they neared.

The interior of this room was nothing like the small prep room they'd used earlier. Lush rugs covered the floor, expensive hangings decorated the walls, and everything was done in a red-and-gold color scheme. There were lots of plump couches, and on one lounged a beautiful woman with a fall of long, red-and-black hair.

"Tillana, go watch the fights," Hager ordered.

Tillana rose. She was far taller than Nea, with generous curves, and wearing barely any clothes. She pulled on a translucent wrap and walked out, hips swinging.

"Sit." Hager reclined on a couch and waved a hand.

Nea sat, and Kaden sat beside her.

"What are you looking for, Kaden?" Hager asked.

She controlled her jolt. "He knows who you are?"

Hager smiled. "I know everything."

For a second, his eyes looked fathomless. Like she could see all the star systems he'd ever visited in his eyes.

Cocking his head, Hager studied her. "You aren't a knighthunter like my friend here."

"Knightmaster," she said.

"Makes sense." He looked at Kaden. "Not like you to take on a partner."

"Ti-Lore," Kaden said. "Where is it?"

Hager ran his tongue over his teeth. "Doesn't sound familiar."

"Hager," Kaden snapped. "I won the fight. A deal is a deal."

Hager leaned back. "It's a bad place, my friend."

"It doesn't matter. I need to know where it is."

"I'm guessing the Gek'Dragar have taken someone important to you."

Nea stiffened. "What do you know about the Gek'Dragar?"

"More than I care to," Hager replied. "Ti-Lore is their top prison world. They have a secret facility there." His face turned serious, and there was no sign of the charming fight club owner. "Once there, no one ever leaves."

That wasn't quite true. Alara had escaped.

"Where is it?" Kaden asked again.

Hager nodded. "The Troctos System. I'll send you what I have on its location. It's in Gek'Dragar space."

Kaden nodded. "We guessed as much."

"Ti-Lore was once a lovely world. I remember my father talking about it. Large mountains, with deep, deep ravines. A stunning cliff world. There used to be lots of villages connected by bridges across the ravines." Hager sighed. "It also had massive reserves of a mineral called senum."

Nea sucked in a breath. It had once been very valuable, but it was exceptionally rare now, seeing as it wasn't found very often.

"Senum, the main ingredient of the drug my people used to enslave those compatible to become navigators. It killed my father, and almost killed me." Hager lifted his shirt.

Nea barely controlled her response. The lower part of Hager's midsection was comprised of metal parts and tubes.

By the coward's bones. He'd had most of his organs replaced.

"The Gek'Dragar sold senum to my people. It was highly valuable. They used terrible techniques to mine it. The local inhabitants of Ti-Lore had mined it for years. In small, quality quantities. They developed a substance, a nano-fluid that could eat through the rock and absorb the senum. It made it easy to extract. It meant no miners were put in dangerous conditions. But, if the nano-fluid got out of control, it could eat through entire mountains. Entire mountain ranges."

Nea's gut curdled. She knew where this story was going.

"The Ti-Lores traded with the Gek'Dragar. They revealed their mining techniques." He shrugged. "The Gek'Dragar invaded, took over, and they used the nano-fluid in vast quantities. All they wanted was more senum. It ate away at the planet until mountains collapsed and villages were buried. The Ti-Lores fought back, and the Gek'Dragar nearly annihilated them all." Hager shifted on the cushions. "They also decided that Ti-Lore made an excellent location for their maximum-security prison. One they kept secret, and where they put their high-level, political prisoners."

"We need the location of that prison," Kaden said.

Hager nodded. "I can tell you, but Kaden...don't go there. There is only death on Ti-Lore. The nano-fluid is soaked into the dirt, and it's dangerous. You'll never come back."

Kaden rose, and Nea did, too.

"I appreciate the warning, and the information," Kaden said.

Hager shook his head. "If you care about this woman, don't go to Ti-Lore and sentence her to death."

"Thank you, Hager." Kaden gave one quick nod. "I'll see you next time."

The club owner sighed. "I hope so. You're the best fighter I know." He looked at Nea. "I suspect you'd be good in the cage, too. Good luck. I'll send the information on Ti-Lore to your encrypted account."

KADEN EXITED Slam and waited for Nea. She didn't look at him, scanning the street. Night had well and truly taken over Prozula.

It made the place a lot more dangerous.

He knew he needed to talk to her. He'd been a *gul* earlier. She'd done nothing wrong. He'd taken her—fast and rough—and then he'd reacted badly to one mention of her *gul*-vexed father.

He saw her stiffen.

"Nea?" He scanned the dark street where she was looking. There were a few people still waiting to enter the club. Some people on the corner were blissed out on drugs. Shadows moved in the darkness, but that wasn't unusual.

"I saw a Gek'Dragar," Nea said.

He tensed. "Where?"

"Across the street. In the shadows of that abandoned building. I swear, I saw him watching us, and I saw other Gek'Dragar in the club."

He frowned, but he didn't sense anyone. "There are a few who come to watch the fights. Come on. Let's get to the alley and get back to the *Helios*." He touched her arm, but she pulled away.

"Nea—"

"We'll talk back on the ship."

He followed her, watching the sway of her hips. He loved the way she moved.

She turned into the alley, and something pinged on his senses. He frowned and looked behind him.

He caught a glimpse of a big silhouette across the street, and every muscle tensed. It was a Gek'Dragar.

"Kaden!"

Nea's shout had him whirling. A flash of her blue energy lit up the alleyway.

Two Gek'Dragar were in the alley, waiting for them. They both rushed at her.

She threw the energy ball, her sword forming in her other hand as she lunged to the side.

Gut tightening, Kaden stormed forward. Suddenly, a large body dropped from the building above.

The Gek'Dragar landed on Kaden. They hit the dirty ground in a tangle.

Kaden grunted, the air rushing out of him. His combat implants activated. He rolled, and then caught the Gek'Dragar in a headlock. Anger fueled him.

The alien bucked, trying to get free.

Kaden formed a knife and rammed the glowing red blade into the Gek'Dragar's side. His foe kicked out and made some deep, guttural noises.

Kaden stabbed again. The sounds of fighting were loud behind him.

He had to get to Nea.

The Gek'Dragar rolled, trying to dislodge Kaden. He held on tight. His red energy formed, crackling in the darkness and flowing up his arm. He slammed his hand against the alien's chest.

The Gek'Dragar's muscles strained, and his big body shook. Then he slumped.

Kaden rolled the alien's body off him and leaped up. He saw Nea slam a blue ball of energy into one Gek'Dragar. He flew back into the wall of the building.

She whirled, leaped, and kicked the other Gek'Dragar in the head. Her blue sword sliced through the air, cutting across the alien's chest.

The Gek'Dragar made a choked sound and dropped to the ground. He didn't get back up.

Nea landed—graceful, yet powerful. She caught Kaden's gaze, and smiled.

He smiled back.

Then, the Gek'Dragar leaning against the wall staggered upright. He muttered something that Kaden couldn't make out, and lifted one of his large hands.

He was holding a small device in it.

Gul.

"Nea!" Kaden threw out his arm and took a step forward.

Boom.

The explosion tore through the alley. The force of it lifted Kaden off his feet. He flew backward, the blast of sound roaring in his ears. Orange flames washed over him.

He landed on his side, pain vibrating through him.

Nea. He rolled to his feet.

The wall of one building was damaged, and there was a depression in the ground from the explosion.

"Nea!" He ran forward. One Gek'Dragar body lay on the ground, a burned and twisted mess. Where the one with the explosive device had been standing, there was nothing left.

Kaden moved deeper into the destroyed alley, could feel the heat throbbing off the ground and walls. Panic slicked through his veins.

He searched every shadow, shoving debris out of his way. "Nea." His voice cracked.

She'd been too close to the blast.

His gut tightened in painful knots. "*Nea.*"

She couldn't...be gone.

Kaden dropped to his knees, sucking in air. Every breath hurt.

Images of Nea slashed through his head. Nea scowling, smiling, concentrating, and how she looked when he moved inside her. His chin dropped to his chest.

He felt like all the color had gone from the world. There was nothing left but gray.

"Knighthunter Kaden? Kaden?"

The voice rang through his implant. It was Ensign Noth from the *Helios.*

"You missed check in. Please respond."

Kaden stared at the debris around him and felt like his insides had been ripped out.

"Knighthunter Kaden?"

He closed his eyes. "I'm here."

"Are you and Knightmaster Nea all right? Did you get the intel?"

"We got it."

He couldn't leave here, not without her. "We were attacked by Gek'Dragar."

"Are you all right? We...please hold."

Kaden swallowed and it felt like he had blades in his throat.

"Kaden." Noth's voice again. "Nea just checked in. She said she got separated from you by an explosion. Her comms are damaged, and she could only connect with us."

Kaden's head jerked up. *What?* "She contacted you?"

"Yes."

"She's alive?" Kaden surged upright, filled with energy.

"Yes, she said she dropped into a sewer."

Kaden scanned the ground. Debris littered the alley. He strode forward and kicked at the mess of rubble with his boot.

There.

He stared at the dark hole in the ground. The entry to the sewer.

Without hesitation, he dropped down into the darkness.

He wouldn't believe Nea was alive until he saw her.

CHAPTER FIFTEEN

Nea sat in the sewer tunnel, leaning back against the wall.

Her ears were still ringing, and her body ached all over. Her wrist was badly sprained and throbbing, but her combat implants told her it wasn't broken. Her hip felt like it was on fire.

She licked her lips and tasted soot.

She'd move...soon.

Thank the stars for the sewer hole. She'd spotted it during the fight. When that Gek'Dragar had lifted the bomb, she'd dived and ripped the cover off. She'd only been half in when the explosion had caught her. She'd fallen the rest of the way.

Her head was foggy, and it was hard to think. She was pretty sure she had a concussion. Her implant would be healing that, too, but it would take time.

She shifted and pain ripped up her side.

With a moan, she looked down and saw a piece of metal lodged in her side.

Gul. Fumbling, she gripped the metal. It was slippery with her blood. She yanked it out.

"By the coward's bones..." She heaved in a breath, fighting back dizziness. Nausea swamped her.

I am not going to vomit. I am not going to vomit. The sensation eased, leaving behind the dull throb in her side.

She dropped the metal piece, and it clanked on the floor of the tunnel. She saw the wound bleeding sluggishly, but it wasn't life threatening.

She heard the skitter of something small moving farther down the tunnel. No doubt some critter. Dropping her head back against the wall, she tried to gather up some energy.

How many times had Kaden felt like this? Injured, alone on some distant planet, hunted by his enemies.

Her heart squeezed and her head swam. She wanted Kaden.

Metal scraped against metal, somewhere above her. She'd tried to contact him, but something was blocking her signal. She'd managed to reach the *Helios.*

Kaden would be worried.

More noises. She forced herself to sit up straighter. If it was more Gek'Dragar, she'd need to fight.

A body dropped from above and landed in a crouch nearby. Boots splashed in a puddle of dirty water.

Then Kaden crouched in front of her. His gaze locked on her face, and she could see how harsh it looked in the low light.

"Hey," she murmured.

He cupped one cheek. "Where are you hurt?" His voice wasn't steady.

"My wrist, but it's not broken. I have a laceration to the side." She swallowed. "A mild concussion. I sort of hurt all over." Something she would never have admitted to Kaden Galath just a few days ago.

His gaze was intense, and a muscle ticked in his jaw. He checked her wrist, then probed her side. She did her best to stifle her moan.

"Sorry." His fingers whispered over her jaw. His touch was surprisingly light. "Nea, I thought you were dead."

She flicked her attention up to him. His gaze was churning, and she heard something buried deep in his tone. She knew now that he was a man who didn't often let his true feelings show.

But she saw them now. She covered his hand with hers. Her fingers were still a little shaky too.

"I'm alive, Kaden. And I'm going to be fine."

He turned his hand over, entwining their fingers. He pressed his forehead to hers. "Let me look after you."

"I don't need—"

"*Nea.*"

She swallowed. There was so much emotion in that one word. She saw he needed this.

Maybe she did too.

She nodded.

He slid his arms around her and lifted her. He held her close to his chest.

Red light grew, welling around them. She felt the strength of his power. Then everything blurred.

The dirty sewer was gone, and the bridge of the *Helios* materialized.

"Is she all right?" Captain Attaway asked.

The lights were bright, and Nea closed her eyes.

"Minor injuries and a concussion," Kaden said. "I'll take care of her. Captain, I've sent the coordinates for Ti-Lore to the ship's computer. Set a course, under full cloak."

"Of course. Well done obtaining the intel." The captain's worried gaze was on Nea.

"We'll be heading deeper into Gek'Dragar space," Kaden said. "And we don't know much about this world."

Nea stirred. "And those Gek'Dragar who attacked us...they suspect we're out here, looking for the knightqueen."

"We aren't going to let them find us," Chief Watson said sharply.

"I'll start searching for anything I can find on Ti-Lore," Ensign Noth said, swiping his console. "Based on the coordinates, it looks like it'll be an eight-hour journey at full speed."

"You sure I can't activate our medical bay for Nea?" the captain asked Kaden.

He shook his head. "Thank you. I can take care of her."

Captain Attaway nodded. "You and the knightmaster get some rest."

Kaden strode off the bridge and Nea leaned into him. "I can walk."

"No." He strode down the corridor.

It took her a second to realize that he wasn't heading toward her cabin or his, and she frowned.

He stopped and pressed a palm to a door. When it

opened, humidity hit her, and she realized they were in the captain's pool room.

"You knew about this pool?"

He set her down gently. "I'm a knighthunter, I know everything."

She realized she was still a little shaky. It hit her. She'd come very close to dying in a dirty sewer on an alien planet.

"Hey, Nea." He pressed a finger under her chin. "You're safe now."

"I know. Just an adrenaline crash, and the realization that I almost died."

"That moment is never fun."

She tilted her head, but her vision blurred. She pressed a hand to her temple. "I'm sure you've been there many times before."

"Too many to count."

Her chest squeezed. She didn't like the idea of this man dying. This complicated man who generated so many strong, confusing emotions in her.

He started unfastening her clothes.

"Kaden—"

"Just let me take care of you. We'll get you cleaned up, injuries dealt with, and some food into you." He pulled her jacket and shirt off. "Get in the pool, Nea. Relax."

After he'd stripped her of the rest of her clothes, she walked into the water. It was warm and felt good. She heard the murmur of Kaden's voice and then the smell of food. He was obviously using the small food printer in the corner of the pool room.

She ducked under the water, trying to wash away the scent of dirt and soot.

She wanted to swim, but she was feeling too shaky. She heard the splash of water and turned.

Kaden was entering the water, and her breath hitched.

He was naked. Every muscle on display, along with a very hard cock.

He reached her and pulled her close. He held up a small bottle.

"Turn," he ordered.

She gave him her back. She smelled something citrusy, and then he was massaging shampoo into her hair. She moaned and let him use his strong fingers to knead her scalp.

"This is from Earth," he said. "The scent is something called Eucalyptus."

"I like it."

"Rinse," he said.

She ducked under. She knew the pool filtration would remove the shampoo.

"I want to take a look at your injuries next," he said.

She leaned on the edge of the small pool. She should have felt awkward with both of them naked, but it felt right. He checked her wrist, then the lump on the side of her head.

She winced. "Distract me."

"With what?" He gently probed her skull.

"Your name? If you don't remember your parents, how did you get your name?"

His fingers stilled. "They assign you names in the care houses."

She turned her head. "They gave it to you?"

"I chose Kaden. I had vague memories of someone calling me that." He shrugged. "Mostly I insisted on it, because I wanted it to be my decision."

She smiled. "That, I believe." And she could imagine a small, frightened, but brave boy insisting on picking his own name. "And Galath?"

"They assigned me that." He paused, gently kneading her hair. "Because I'm Galatine."

Nea went very still. It was something so rare that it was more legend than reality. "What?"

"You know my powers are...different. The care home realized it very quickly. I was given extra training to learn to harness my abilities."

Galatine were very rare Oronis knights. As far as she knew, history had only recorded the existence of a few of them. Dark knights with deadly powers that were unleashed on the enemies of the Oronis.

Knights who were often feared because of their power.

"I have a rare mutation that gives me different, more powerful abilities. Just like the Galatine of old."

He pressed his palm against the ragged cut on her side. Warmth tingled over her skin.

Her eyebrows winged up. "You can heal?" Usually, only knighthealers could do that.

"Only a little. And only on very minor wounds."

She looked down at her side. The cut was half healed, and didn't hurt anymore.

Yes, he had so many secrets. But she realized now that she trusted him.

He put up an arrogant, unfeeling façade, but he was a loyal knight to the bone. One who fought for and protected the Oronis.

Who fought for and protected her.

"I guess that makes you special, Kaden."

He snorted. "Hardly."

She cupped his jaw. "I think so."

She saw him swallow. "It makes me dangerous. My powers..." He looked away.

He'd always been so overconfident that it was strange to see the flash of uncertainty.

He touched her wound again, his touch impossibly gentle. "You can't get hurt, Nea."

She shivered at the fierceness in his voice.

"I won't allow it." His voice was sharp. "Today, I came too close to losing you."

Tears welled in her eyes, and she tried to hide them. Crying wasn't allowed in her household.

"Shh." Kaden's thumbs brushed the tears away.

"I never cry," she said.

"Cry if you want to. I'll hold you."

"Knights do not cry. I can't fall apart."

"Says who?"

"My father. I'm a Laurier. I have to be strong, have no faults, be perfect."

Kaden made an annoyed sound. "Your gul-vexed father can..." Kaden shook his head. "Cry, and lean on me. You're dealing with your feelings and emotions from what happened. It makes you stronger to deal with them, not weaker." He gave her a wry smile. "Or so I'm told."

She let out a sob, and he wrapped his arms around her. She held on to him, cried. The last time she'd cried was when her brother had died. She'd cried alone in the shower and never let anyone see.

With Kaden's strong arms around her, her tears eased quickly.

"Earlier, in Slam, when I mentioned my father—"

"It's okay. I overreacted."

"No. What I meant... He approves of no one. Least of all me."

Kaden's brows drew together. "I thought... You're his daughter. He must be proud."

"My mother died, then my brother. He changed. Turned harsher and more unforgiving. Nothing I do ever lives up to his standards."

Kaden growled. "Then he's a bigger idiot than I thought he was."

She let out a laugh.

Their bodies moved closer, brushing against each other.

She saw something change in Kaden's gaze. "*Nea.*"

She kissed him.

But this time the kiss was slower, lingered longer. There was no quick ignition of heat like all the other times they'd come together. It was a lazy, long exploration. And perhaps comfort, as well.

She slid her hands in his hair, and the kiss deepened. His fingers gripped her hips.

He groaned into her mouth.

Yes. She felt his hard cock pulsing against her belly. "Kaden, I need you."

Something flashed in his eyes. Then he lifted her into his arms and walked out of the pool.

KADEN CARRIED Nea out of the pool, holding her like she was precious.

He needed her. He suspected they both needed this. He wouldn't rush it this time. He wouldn't hurt her.

He lowered her to the large, plush lounging pillows beside the pool.

After taking a second to appreciate the picture she made, he laid down beside her, and kissed her. It was long and deep. He could think of nothing but her.

He let his lips travel to the side of her head, and gently kissed the scrape there. He lifted her arm, and kissed her sore wrist. Then he moved lower, kissing across her jaw, her collarbone, one breast. He heard her breath hitch.

He found more scrapes, and let his lips drift over them. When he reached the almost-healed wound on her side, he let his kiss turn even more gentle.

"I don't like you hurt," he murmured.

She tugged on his hair. "Make me forget, Kaden. Give me something better to focus on."

He crawled up her body, gently lowering himself between her hips.

There was a flash of the heat that always sparked

between them, but this time it was tempered by something softer. Something deeper and warmer.

He cupped her breasts. She made a breathy sound and pushed into his palms.

He thumbed her nipples, and she pressed against him. He traced his fingers over her collarbone, seeing pure desire in her eyes.

"I need you," she whispered.

His heart thudded. Words he'd never known he'd been waiting to hear from her.

He moved lower, pushing her legs wider apart. Hunger welled in his gut. He'd never deny this woman anything.

He moved his hand down her belly, to the juncture of her thighs. He stroked her and found her already slick. He thrust a finger inside her and listened to the sounds she made.

Keeping his eyes on her, he lowered his head. Her chest hitched, and he smiled.

He pressed kisses to her core. Her body arched up, but he held her down. He licked, then found that swollen nub and sucked. Nea cried out, panting hard, one of her hands gripping his hair.

"I need you inside me, Kaden," she gasped.

He couldn't wait any longer. He shifted and notched the head of his cock between her legs. He slid home, watching her face.

She bit her lip and murmured his name.

He pulled out, and thrust back in. He found a steady rhythm that had her clutching at his back.

Connected. Being connected like this, he felt closer

than he ever had to anyone.

He could've lost her.

He focused on the feel of her. She was right here. She was tight around him. He kept thrusting, and soon he felt her tense, her inner muscles clamping down on his cock.

So beautiful. She cried out and he watched her come, fighting back his own release with vicious control.

He felt her nails scratch his back, and he liked it. He wanted her marks.

"*Kaden.*"

"Again." He picked up the pace. He still felt driven to make sure she was okay, to prove that she was alive. "I want you to come again, my gorgeous Nea."

Her cheeks were flushed.

He kept thrusting, his spine tingling. He wouldn't last much longer. He slid a hand between their slick bodies and stroked her.

"Oh, stars. I—" She broke apart again, her cry echoing in the room.

This time, her release triggered his own. With a deep groan, Kaden thrust deep and came inside.

Chest heaving, he fell forward, shifting to lie beside her. He curled around her, her body in the shelter of his.

"Okay?" He pressed a kiss to the side of her head.

She nodded. "I feel much better."

He suspected she was still tired and achy, but he knew after some sleep, Knightmaster Nea would pull herself together. She was the strongest person he knew. He nuzzled her hair.

He'd been alone all his life.

He'd come from nothing, kept his connections

limited. People had come and gone so quickly in his life. Most of them he was better off without. Ashtin was the only person truly close to him. As a knighthunter, it was perfect to never let anyone in, never let anyone matter.

Nea changed that.

He released a breath and breathed her in. Maybe he'd always known she'd been more to him. From the first moment he'd seen her. That was why he tried to keep a wedge between them at the Academy, to stop her from being his greatest weakness. And to protect her.

Whatever happened, Nea Laurier was his.

His to protect. His to kill for, if he had to. And, if necessary, his to die for.

CHAPTER SIXTEEN

It was a gentle stroke on her face that woke her.

Nea opened her eyes. Kaden was crouched beside the bed in her cabin. He was in his armor.

After their frenzied lovemaking by the pool, he'd carried her to her cabin. Then, despite his protests, she'd climbed on top of him and taken him that time.

It was her new favorite pastime, driving Kaden Galath past his control and watching him come. After that, they'd slept.

"It's time?" she asked.

"It's time," he confessed. "We've reached Ti-Lore."

She sat up.

"How are you feeling?" he asked.

"Good." She'd slept well in his arms. "Everything feels much better. I'll take a stim, just in case." A stimulant would give her an extra boost to complete the mission.

And bring the knightqueen home.

"I'll meet you on the bridge." He kissed her, taking

his time, like he couldn't quite pull himself away. Then he left her to get ready.

Nea used the washroom, and soon was dressed in her armor. She finished braiding her hair and drew in a deep breath.

She was going on a dangerous mission with Kaden Galath.

And there was no one else she wanted at her side.

After this was over, they needed to work out what the *gul* was between them. Because things had drastically changed. The man she hated...

She shook her head. She didn't have time for this right now.

When she strode onto the bridge, the atmosphere was tense. Captain Attaway glanced over, her mouth bracketed by tight lines.

"Nea," the captain said.

"Captain." Nea's gaze moved to the viewscreen.

"You're feeling better."

Nea nodded.

Ti-Lore looked pretty from space. The peaks of vast mountain ranges bisected the planet. The north and south poles were covered in dense greenery. Across the middle, the planet was all shades of brown.

"It doesn't look too bad from here," Ensign Noth said. "I sent a probe down."

New images appeared on the screen, and Nea sucked in a sharp breath.

Mighty mountains that had collapsed. Some looked like they'd imploded from the inside, while others looked as though they'd been partly eaten away by some giant creature. As the probe zoomed through a ravine, she saw old bridges—decayed, broken, hanging down. There were also abandoned villages cut into the cliff faces. They were crumbling from disuse and neglect.

She wanted to believe that the people who'd once lived here had gotten away, but she knew that probably wasn't the truth.

Here was another world destroyed by the Gek'Dragar, and their greed and ambition.

The probe flew lower into the ravine. Deep in the shadowed darkness, shapes were moving. Her gaze narrowed. *What was that?*

Beside her, Kaden cursed.

That's when the silhouettes came into focus. They were...monsters. Massive creatures, snarling and fighting. One had horns and huge claws; it swiped at another that looked misshapen and colossal.

"The nano-fluid," the ensign said quietly. "It mutated the planet's native animals."

The captain shook her head.

"The Ti-Lores were a peaceful humanoid species." The next image showed two tall men with red skin, black hair, and long, aristocratic faces. "There aren't many left."

Nea clasped her hands together and fought back her anger.

"We need to start a grid search to find the Gek'-Dragar prison," Kaden said. "Hager's intel gave an approximate area."

The ensign smiled. "I already found it."

Nea straightened. "How?"

"I figured I'd check for large energy signatures. The Ti-Lores didn't use vast amounts of energy, and like I said, there aren't many of them left. Any survivors mostly live in small villages on the flats near the sea, away from the nano-fluid-riddled mountains. I assumed that a prison would be using a lot of power, and would be easy to zero in on. Once I narrowed down the location, I noted that the bridges and mountain paths in the area were in good repair. Someone's maintaining and using them."

"Well done, Noth," Kaden said.

On the screen, an image of a dramatic spiked, triangular peak appeared.

It was stunning, but as Nea looked closer, she noted a structure at a lower level, with a bridge reaching across a deep ravine. The prison was built into the mountainside.

"Scans show that the entire mountain peak is hollow," the ensign said.

Nea's stomach clenched. "It's all one giant prison."

"Most likely," Kaden said.

"I can't risk getting the probe too close. But it looks like there's only one bridge leading in."

On the screen, Nea watched supplies being delivered to a staging area at the base of the prison. Gek'Dragar guards were unloading containers.

"The prison is using a lot of energy," the ensign continued. "I suspect most of it is to repel the nano-fluid that's present in the mountains, and for monitoring systems. So no one can get in."

"And no one can get out." Nea pressed her hands to her hips. "So how do we get into the prison?"

Kaden stared at the screen. "We sneak across the

bridge and hide in the supplies. Let them carry us inside."

Nea watched the Gek'Dragar hefting containers onto floating sleds, then pushing them into the prison. "But how do we get across the bridge? They have patrols. And no doubt cameras and sensors will be focused on it."

"On the *top* of it." Kaden turned to her. "So we go in *under* it."

Nea frowned. "Risky, but it could work."

He smiled. "I think I've corrupted the sensible Nea Laurier."

She smiled back. "Maybe you have."

And she found that she didn't mind that very much. These days with Kaden, in the middle of this intense, dangerous mission, with the highest stakes of her life, she realized that she'd felt...alive.

She'd felt pushed and challenged. And she'd felt cared for. She trusted Kaden to have her back.

Her throat tightened. She'd never had that. Her father's love had always been contingent on so many things. Things she never lived up to, according to him.

Kaden saw her just as she was, and he liked her just as she was.

Oh, stars. She felt a tremor inside. Maybe she didn't hate him as much as she thought she did.

How had the man she'd loathed and distrusted for so long become so important to her?

"Nea?"

She looked at him.

His blue eyes glittered. "Are you ready to rescue our queen?"

She gave him a brisk nod. "Let's do it."

THEY TELEPORTED INTO A RUINED, abandoned village.

After ensuring Nea was steady after the transport, Kaden looked around.

The dwellings had been cut into the cliff. He figured this had once been a busy and thriving place, but now, there was nothing but ghosts.

Walls had crumbled, rubble lay strewn in the walkways, the wind whistled through the empty homes.

Nea wandered around and crouched. Then she picked up something. He saw a small carved object on her palm. A child's toy.

She rose and shook her head. "The Gek'Dragar have hurt so many. They take, destroy, steal, and kill. To make their own species *greater*." She shook her head again, and set the toy down on a half-crumbled wall. "They need to be stopped."

"I agree."

"Today, we rescue the knightqueen, but this fight is not over. We have to ensure the Gek'Dragar don't destroy more worlds."

There was a promise in her words. He'd always admired Nea's drive to protect and defend others.

"But first, we need to free Carys and Sten." Kaden walked to the edge of the cliff. The old railing was crumbling, and he was careful not to get too close to the edge. Debris crunched under his boots.

He looked up at the peak of the mountain looming above. He could see the underside of the bridge. He drew in a deep breath. Carys and Sten were here; he could sense it.

Nea moved up beside him, her arm brushing his.

"They're here," Kaden said. "I'm certain of it."

She nodded and looked up, determination on her face. "Let's go and get them."

The two of them moved stealthily out of the village. They snuck up a narrow, mountain path toward the bridge. A misty rain started to fall, and he scowled. It would make it slippery. But as he watched, visibility across the ravine dropped. That could help hide them.

All of a sudden, the ground vibrated faintly under Kaden's feet. He stilled.

"There's a transport coming," she hissed.

There weren't many places to hide. He spotted a boulder blocking the path ahead, and he hurried to it. He crouched down and Nea slid in beside him. He pulled her close.

Their armor changed color to match the rock.

The rumble of the engine grew louder. He glanced down over the edge of the path. There was a wider road cut into the cliff on a lower level. A ground transport with large tires lumbered up the hill. The back of it was loaded with crates.

"Supply drop," Nea said quietly.

They stayed still and watched the transport follow the road up to the bridge. As it moved across, the bridge swayed.

Kaden angled his head and studied the Gek'Dragar

guards on the bridge, scanning around as the transport crossed. He also noticed a security bot on the bridge, as well.

It was roughly spherical, made of brown metal, with several attachments to it. He knew it would have sensors and weapons.

They'd need to avoid that.

"Come on," he murmured.

He and Nea continued upward. The path brought them to right under the bridge. He could see some parts were made of older rope, but the rest of it had been reinforced with metal. The Gek'Dragar had probably patched up an old Ti-Lore bridge with new materials.

"All right, let's go," he said.

The rain was still falling, but wasn't too heavy. Kaden gripped the underside of the cables and swung out.

His legs dangled under him, and he looked down. He steeled himself. The ravine was deep. The bottom was only a dark shadow, far, far away.

A drop would kill them.

He lifted his feet up, and used his combat implant to create hooks on the end of his boots. He hooked them into the bridge.

"Nea?"

She followed him, climbing out under the bridge and getting into position.

Kaden reached out and started moving. He picked his handholds carefully, and took his time.

There was no room for error.

They edged across the bridge. Water dripped down, running across his visor.

You okay?

He sent the message via his implant.

I'm fine.

He glanced back. She looked strong and capable. His chest swelled. She was amazing. Her father was an idiot for not seeing that.

Soon, he judged they were about halfway across. Suddenly, guttural conversation rumbled above them.

He froze.

The Gek'Dragar were close.

Kaden and Nea.

It was a message from the *Helios*.

The probe has picked up several guards on the bridge. And a security bot. They are almost at your location.

He saw Nea freeze, and they waited.

The bridge vibrated. Through the tiny gaps, he saw boots appear.

Kaden kept his breathing slow and easy. His fingers tightened on the ropes. He heard a beeping sound, and then he saw the security bot floating across the bridge.

He gave a mental curse. It would be running security scans.

If it scanned downward...

But it had no reason to do that. Thankfully, it seemed to just be focused above the bridge.

Nea, stay still. Use your implant to slow your breathing and heartbeat.

Acknowledged.

He watched the bot roll over him.

A Gek'Dragar guard walked behind it. The minutes ticked by, and the bot and the guard continued on.

Kaden blew out a breath.

We're clear. Let's move.

He reached for the next handhold and got a good grip.

Let's move quickly before that patrol comes back.

The message from Nea projected across his visor.

Agreed.

Soon, they reached the other side of the bridge. There was a short climb up to the top of the bridge. The rain had stopped.

He looked at Nea and she nodded. He found foot and hand holds in the steep cliff face, and climbed up it.

At the top, he crouched, keeping low, and scanned the area in front of the base. Nea was right behind him. He heard guards talking near the entrance, but couldn't see them.

"Kaden." Nea kept her voice low and tapped his shoulder. "There."

He saw a large container nearby with the lid open.

He nodded.

They quickly both ran. Kaden gripped the edge and vaulted into the container. Nea climbed inside after him. Kaden closed the lid, locking them in darkness.

Now, they waited.

CHAPTER SEVENTEEN

Nea pressed her hands on the side of the container as it rocked and jolted.

It wasn't the smoothest ride.

Beside her, Kaden braced his body against hers. They were being transported inside.

Just a little bit longer.

Finally, the rocking stopped, and everything went quiet. Kaden took her hand and squeezed.

Let's go.

His message scrolled across her visor and she nodded.

He reached up and cracked open the container lid. He peered through.

"Clear," he whispered. He pushed open the lid the rest of the way, and climbed out.

Nea rose and clambered carefully out of the container.

They were in a dark room, filled with rows and rows of stacked containers.

"It looks like a storage room," he said.

"Where to now?" They didn't know the layout of the prison, so they'd have to plan as they went.

"Where would you put your highest value prisoner?"

Nea paused. "In this prison? Right at the top."

"Agreed. We get to the top and find our queen."

Kaden moved like a wraith. Silent like the shadows themselves. She followed him out into a rough corridor. The walls were hewn from dark-gray rock, the floors were uneven.

They needed to find some stairs. They continued on and reached a junction. There were several corridors, and Kaden paused and listened. He jerked his head, and they went left. As a knighthunter, his senses were more acute and attuned than hers.

Suddenly, he stopped. He pulled her flush against the wall.

Now, she heard the thud of heavy footsteps. Her heart thumped. They stayed still and she heard several Gek'Dragar pass by the junction. The sound faded.

Kaden pointed and they moved forward. They continued down the corridor. Nea looked at some of the rooms and saw they looked like quarters for the guards. Then she spotted the stairs and grabbed Kaden's arm.

Together, they moved upward. The stairs were rough and uneven in places.

The next level was another warren of corridors. A sharp scream echoed from above, filled with pain and terror. She froze. It echoed off the walls.

Gul. She gritted her teeth. The scream was followed by moans and sobbing.

The sounds of despair.

Kaden's face was a blank mask, but a muscle ticked beside his mouth. He pointed upward.

They continued up the stairs. Each level became narrower and narrower.

"Kaden." She pointed at a comp console built into the wall. Its lights gleamed in the gloom.

After a quick scan around, he pressed his palm against it. As he interfaced with it, she watched data fill the screen.

"There are only a few prisoners." His face hardened. "Four of them. They've been tortured extensively, and are listed as not surviving much longer. Their injuries are too severe."

Nea looked at the floor, her heart heavy. "And the knightqueen and Sten?"

"Not listed. But there are two new high-priority prisoners marked as having just arrived."

Her head jerked up. "It's them."

"Yes. Let's get to the top."

They continued on. A few more times, they had to stop and hide from the guards.

"We must be getting closer," Kaden said.

Soon. Soon they'd find Carys and Sten.

The next level was filled with prison cells. A thick silence filled the space, except for a pained moan from deep within. She closed her eyes and wished they could rescue everyone, even knowing how badly injured they were.

They deserved freedom. Even for only a little while.

At the next level, the stairs stopped. There were no windows in this room. It was an open space, filled only with stone pillars that disappeared into the darkness. Water was dripping somewhere.

"We aren't at the top yet." Kaden frowned. "There must be more stairs somewhere."

Nea stepped forward.

Deeper in the room she heard the sound of scraping. It sounded like something large. The hairs on the back of her neck rose.

A low sound filled the room—part moan, part growl.

Gul, there was something in here. "Kaden..."

"*Shh.*"

There was another scraping sound, and her pulse sped up.

A chain clanked.

Thump. Thump. Thump.

The creature appeared out of the gloomy murk. It was ten feet tall, its head almost brushing the ceiling. Its body looked over-developed, with red skin stretched taut over bulging muscles like someone had overstuffed it.

It stepped forward, its arms flexing. There was a chain around its neck like a collar. It lifted its head. It had no hair and small, milky eyes. It sniffed. Rows of needle-like teeth filled its mouth.

It kept sniffing.

Kaden pointed at her and pressed a finger to his lips. Nea moved right, and he moved left.

The creature's blind.

Nea agreed with Kaden's assessment.

But it looks like it relies on its sense of smell.

There was something familiar about it. The red skin...

By the coward's bones. *Kaden, I think it's a mutated Ti-Lore.*

Gul.

What had once been a Ti-Lore had clearly been affected by the nano-fluid. The poor soul. She felt a rush of sympathy, and a surge of anger.

The Gek'Dragar had done this.

They'd abused the nano-fluid, and sentenced this person to a monstrous life. Using him, after ruining his planet.

She vowed it would end. Her fingers curled, her nails cutting into her palm. She would fight as long as it took to stop the Gek'Dragar.

She took another step, and her boot hit a small rock. It rolled across the floor.

The creature swiveled and roared.

"Nea, run!" Kaden yelled.

The creature's head swiveled again in the direction of Kaden's voice. Nea sprinted forward, then heard the monster charge after her.

Gul, it was fast.

She zigzagged and it roared. She ducked behind a pillar. It was right behind her.

"Hey! Over here."

At Kaden's shout, the creature stopped and swiveled.

Nea turned, her chest heaving. The creature was sniffing, and zeroing in on Kaden. It charged again, pumping its arms and legs.

Her heart leaped into her throat. Kaden dived to the

side and rolled. Then he was back on his feet, racing toward her.

She sent a message across the comm.

How do we kill it?

I'm not sure.

The monster bellowed. She heard shouts of the Gek'-Dragar guards echoing up the stairwell.

Gul.

They were about to have company. Unwanted company.

Then the creature charged toward them again. It ran through a pillar, pulverizing it. Rock flew everywhere.

"Go!" Kaden shouted.

Nea turned and ran.

STONE EXPLODED EVERYWHERE.

The creature had taken out several pillars. Kaden pulled energy toward him, red forming on his hands.

Nea, hide.

At his message, he saw her dart across the room and crouch behind a pillar. The mutated creature took two lumbering steps toward her, swiveling its head, searching.

Kaden tossed a red energy spike.

The creature moved at the last second, and the energy hit a pillar. Rock flew everywhere. The monster roared, whirled, and charged his way.

Kaden sprinted to the side. The monster gave chase.

He whirled behind another pillar. As the creature lumbered closer, he heard its raspy breaths. Kaden felt a rush of sympathy for the man it had once been. No one deserved this.

It got closer, taking some deep sniffs.

Kaden stayed very still. He heard the creature's breathing, sensed its bulk. Hot, fetid breath washed over him. *Gul.*

Suddenly, a ball of blue energy hit the creature.

It staggered backward, clawing at its chest. Kaden turned his head and saw Nea standing in the darkness, blue light on her hands.

We have company.

At her warning, he turned.

Gek'Dragar guards were cresting the stairs.

They lifted their large blasters and fired. Laser fire lit up the darkness.

Kaden ran at them, and teleported. He reappeared right in front of them, and threw several energy spikes into the ceiling.

Crack.

Rock rained down, covering the stairs, and cutting off the path for more reinforcements.

Three Gek'Dragar remained in the room. They swiveled their weapons toward him.

Kaden morphed his swords. Red energy ignited along their blades. He leaped into the air, swords swinging. The blades cut across the chest of the closest Gek'Dragar. Blood spurted and the guard dropped.

Landing with a bend of his knees, Kaden pivoted and kicked a second attacker, then sliced his sword across the neck of the third.

He turned, just in time to see the final Gek'Dragar guard's face contort.

With terror.

He was looking past Kaden.

Without thinking, Kaden dropped and rolled.

The mutant creature charged in, narrowly missing stepping on Kaden. The monster grabbed the remaining Gek'Dragar and lifted the guard into the air. The man screamed. The creature bashed him against the floor. It did it again and again.

Kaden rose and backed up. He spotted Nea and hurried over to her.

"Are you all right?" he whispered, touching her cheek.

She nodded. She looked at where the creature was turning the guard to pulp. "Except we're stuck in here with that thing and no way out."

"First thing, we take it down."

"Put it out of its misery." Her blue sword formed in her hand.

Kaden lifted his own curved swords.

"We work together." He smiled. "Think you can do that?"

"Surprisingly, I don't mind working with you."

All sound stopped. They both turned and stood shoulder to shoulder.

The creature stood facing them, muscular arms

hanging at its sides. Its chest rose and fell. Its hands and face were covered in blood.

It stomped its foot, then broke into a run. It burst through more pillars.

Gul, too many more and the entire ceiling would collapse.

"Now!" Kaden yelled.

The two of them split, their swords whirling. As Kaden went high, Nea went low, cutting across the creature's legs.

Its enraged roar rattled the walls.

Kaden walked backward, crossing his swords, then swinging his arms wide. His blades cut into the thick skin. The creature's blood was a sickly, black color.

Nea jumped, and rammed her sword into its back.

It went wild, shaking its head and swinging its arms.

Kaden dived, then tackled Nea out of the way.

They rose, standing close to the far wall. They were now trapped between unforgiving stone, and the creature.

It lifted its head and bared its teeth. It was bleeding and hurt, but it wasn't down.

Kaden ignited an energy ball. Nea's sword dissolved and her bow formed. The energy bolt notched in it glowed blue. Her face was set. No fear, just resolute dedication.

Kaden tossed his energy. Nea let loose with a bolt.

They hit the creature, and it roared again. Kaden watched the energy eating away at its skin.

It charged, sprinting at them. Nea ran to the right and

Kaden to the left. The monster took out more pillars, and a chunk of the roof collapsed, rock raining down.

A large piece of rubble hit Kaden's head, and he grunted. He threw his arms up.

"*Kaden.*" Nea reached him.

"I'm okay." He turned, fighting back the pain in his head.

Part of the ceiling and wall were gone. Daylight streamed in, backlighting the creature. Its chest worked like a bellows.

Beyond the opening lay the deep ravine.

He met Nea's gaze.

She raised her bow and nodded.

Kaden pulled his energy to him, letting it grow. It came, eager and strong. It welled from deep inside him. From a place he usually kept locked up.

But today he needed the extra power. Today, he had to protect Nea.

Together, they walked toward the beast.

Nea released energy bolt after energy bolt. Kaden's red energy spikes hit the creature's midsection.

It halted, body jerking with each blow.

"Keep firing," Kaden said.

He and Nea advanced, not giving up, or slowing down.

The creature took one step back, then another. Its sightless gaze met theirs, and he saw horror and agony etched on its face.

Go now. Find peace.

Kaden's next spike glowed deep red. He felt another sharp pain, this time at the base of his skull as he fired.

The energy hit the creature mid-chest. Potent red energy crawled over the alien's skin.

It let out a moan.

The creature took another step, then stumbled back through the hole. It let out a roar and fell into the ravine.

CHAPTER EIGHTEEN

Clasping her bleeding arm, Nea staggered to Kaden. "Are you all right?"

He looked terrible. Blood soaked his pale hair, and ran down the side of his neck. He'd been hit by falling rubble.

"I'll live." He took a step closer and almost fell.

She caught him against her, her mouth going dry. "*Kaden.*"

"I took a hard knock to the head." He touched the back of his neck. "I think my oralite implant is damaged."

She sucked in a breath. "Damaged?"

"I can't fully access my implants." His mouth flattened, his face stark. "I can't use my energy. I can't make any energy or weapons."

Oh, no. "Can you teleport?"

He paused, then shook his head.

She ran a hand through her hair. "It doesn't matter. You're a knighthunter. You're Knighthunter Kaden Galath, and you're deadly and skilled."

All knights trained with and without their implants for situations just like this.

A rhythmic pounding sounded from below, vibrating through the floor, and she frowned.

"The Gek'Dragar are trying to find a way in," he said.

Gul. "Then we need to hurry and find the knightqueen."

Nea strode straight to the hole ripped into the side of the prison. The wind whipped in, catching her hair. The remnants of dramatic mountains ringed the valley, but her gaze dropped down to the deep, deep crevasse.

Then she looked up and her heart stopped. "Kaden, look."

He stepped up beside her. He wasn't moving in his usual fluid way. She knew he was hurt and in pain. Without his oralite functioning properly, he couldn't block pain, and couldn't heal.

She pointed to the set of stairs carved into the outside of the prison. They led up to the next level.

"After you, Knightmaster," he said.

She stepped out onto a narrow ledge and shuffled over toward the stairs. Kaden was right behind her.

They reached the stairs and she hauled herself over the railing. She started upward. The stairs were wet and slick, and the wind howled around them. They followed the curve upward. Above, she saw windows cut into the rock and covered by metal bars.

There was a door at the top of the stairs.

They stopped. Carys and Sten were here, she was sure of it. *So close.*

Nea drew in a breath and formed her sword.

Kaden had no weapon, but his gaze was narrowed, and he looked ready to fight.

"For the knightqueen," she said.

"For the knightqueen." His gaze traced over her face. "And for the most beautiful, competent knightmaster I know."

Her heart swelled. Then Kaden stepped back, lifted a foot, and kicked the door in.

There were two Gek'Dragar guards inside. Nea threw an energy blast at one, then attacked the other with her sword.

He growled at her, reaching for his weapon.

She cut him down.

She lifted her head, and watched Kaden land vicious kicks and hits on the other guard. The Gek'Dragar fell under the onslaught.

Kaden leaned down and snatched up a Gek'Dragar blaster.

Suddenly, a low *whoop whoop* sound echoed from below—rhythmic and constant.

"Alarm," he said.

The Gek'Dragar knew they were coming for the queen. They would throw everything at them.

"We need to get the queen and get out of here," Nea said.

They turned toward the metal door to the lone cell. It had a huge lock on it.

"See if there's a key on the guards," she said.

Kaden quickly rifled through the Gek'Dragar's belts. "Here." He took a rectangular key and handed it to her.

She shoved it into the lock and turned it. With a beep, it unlocked, and she shoved the door open.

She stared at the empty cell.

"*No.*" She blinked, her stomach dropping.

There were carved stone benches along the walls, but other than that, it was empty. No Carys, and no Sten.

Kaden cursed, then he strode forward. The bars on the window were bent.

There was just enough space for a body to squeeze through.

He turned, scanning the cell. Something caught his eye and he snatched it up off the floor. He held it up. It was a piece of tattered, gold fabric.

"From Knightqueen Carys' dress," Nea said. "They were here."

He nodded. "They used the commotion to escape." He gave a harsh laugh. "This is the only time I don't like Sten's unwavering devotion to keeping the knightqueen safe."

"They can't have gone far. We'll find them."

Kaden stepped up and looked out the barred window. "There are some handholds carved into the rock below. They must be climbing down the cliff face into the ravine."

When he stepped back, Nea leaned forward and looked as well. Her stomach did a sickening turn. It looked slippery and treacherous. "We need to find them."

Kaden nodded. "Let's go—"

The thunder of many pairs of boots rose behind them.

Nea swiveled. A group of Gek'Dragar was jogging up the external stairs.

"*Gul*. The Gek'Dragar are here. Lots of them."

Kaden lifted the Gek'Dragar weapon. "Let's do what we do best. And give Carys and Sten time to get away."

Nea turned, ready to fight.

GEK'DRAGAR STORMED THROUGH THE DOOR.

Kaden fired his stolen weapon. Nea had formed her bow again, firing with powerful precision.

But this prison was full of Gek'Dragar guards. They'd keep coming.

He cursed in his head. If only he could teleport them out. He tried to access his oralite implant again. Blinding pain spiked through his head.

He staggered and almost dropped his weapon. A Gek'Dragar used the moment to run at him.

The big body slammed into him, and they crashed to the floor.

"Kaden!"

He tried to roll, but pain reverberated through his body. The Gek'Dragar got on top of him and gripped his neck. Those large hands pressed and squeezed.

Kaden saw a flash of blue. Nea threw an energy ball at the door. Over his attacker's shoulder, and he saw several Gek'Dragar fall off the stairs.

Then Nea was standing over him, blue sword in hand.

She rammed it down, sinking into the guard's shoulder. She pushed harder.

The guard's face turned into an ugly grimace, blood running down his chest. He slumped and Kaden pushed the body away.

Nea's gaze met his. "Kaden?"

Suddenly, a huge Gek'Dragar ran through the door. He was holding a large hammer. He swung at her, and the weapon slammed into Nea's side.

"No!" Kaden bellowed.

She flew sideways and hit the wall.

Rage washed through Kaden. He leaped on the Gek'-Dragar. They grappled, but Kaden was fueled by fear and anger for Nea. He wrenched the hammer away from the guard.

The Gek'Dragar gave him a burning look filled with hate.

Kaden adjusted his grip and swung the hammer.

Bone crunched. With a groan, the Gek'Dragar dropped to the floor. Kaden swung again. Two more heavy blows knocked the Gek'Dragar out. He went still.

Chest heaving, Kaden dropped the hammer. He raced to the door and slammed it shut. He flicked the lock into place.

A second later, a heavy weight hit it from the outside. Gek'Dragar hammered at it.

It wouldn't hold them for long.

He limped to Nea and crouched. She was sitting against the wall.

"Nea?" He cupped her cheeks. She was covered in dirt and blood. He heard her pained breaths.

"I am...okay."

"No, you're not." He touched her side.

She cried out.

Kaden bit off a curse. "He broke several ribs."

"My implant is blocking the worst of it."

"Internal bleeding?"

She looked away. "I'm fine."

She wasn't fine. She needed medical attention. There was only so much her implants could do for significant injuries.

Pain scored his insides. The knightqueen was missing. Nea was hurt. Kaden couldn't use his powers.

He wanted to roar out his frustration.

The outside door vibrated again.

"Come on." He helped her up. Every small moan she made stabbed at him.

He scooped up another Gek'Dragar blaster, and kept one arm around her as they hobbled back into the cell. He slammed the door closed behind them.

"I know you're hurting, but you need to climb out through the bars, then climb down the cliff," he said.

She shook her head. "I'm too hurt, Kaden. I'll fall. Besides, the Gek'Dragar will fire on me. They'll pick me off."

He gritted his teeth. He *would* save her. There was no other option.

"Your oralite?" she asked.

He released a sharp breath and tried to access it. Pain cut through his head and down to the base of his skull, but he gritted his teeth and tried harder.

"Kaden, stop."

Nea cupped his face and swiped his upper lip. Blood was dripping from his nose.

"Stop," she whispered.

"Never. Not until you're safe."

"Until the queen is safe."

He shook his head, and stroked his thumb over her lips. "You're my queen, Nea. It's always been you."

Emotion filled her face. *"Kaden."*

He pressed his lips to hers. He tasted blood, but he also tasted Nea. He kissed her, trying to pour everything he felt for her into it.

All of a sudden, a mechanical whirr hummed beyond the cell. He swiveled. A security bot floated up outside the bars. It fired, hitting the rock wall. Rock chips flew everywhere.

Kaden shoved Nea to the side. He jerked the Gek'-Dragar weapon up and fired.

The bot shuddered, and fell to the side. Then it dropped like a rock. He watched it hit the rocky cliff below, and shatter.

A deafening crash beyond the cell door told him the Gek'Dragar had burst through the outer door.

They didn't have much time.

"Nea, go. I'll hold them off and give you time to get away."

"You'll sacrifice yourself for me." She closed the distance between them. "Like all those times you went on missions, and broke the rules and risked your life for intel that would help my missions?"

He stilled. "Nea—"

"I know, Kaden. You've done it for years."

"To protect you." He took another step, so their bodies brushed. "Don't you realize, I'd do anything for you?"

"I know." She grabbed his face and kissed him.

She kissed him like there was nothing but the two of them. He held her to him, careful not to squeeze her injured ribs.

She kept kissing him, like he was the most important thing in her world.

When she pulled back, her gaze was fierce. "We're leaving together. You and me. Kaden and Nea."

He cupped her jaw. "*Nea—*"

"Together. I'd do anything for you too. I choose you, Kaden."

CHAPTER NINETEEN

Nea stared at the man who'd changed everything.

Once, she'd believed that she'd hated him. But working with him, being with him, she'd uncovered so many layers that she'd never seen before.

That he'd never let her see, until now.

She brushed her lips against his. "I need you."

His fingers clamped on her hip. "Nea."

"This doesn't mean I like you," she whispered. "It means I love you."

She saw that very-rare, shocked look on his face, and the fierce emotion that filled his ice-blue eyes.

"No one's ever said that to me before," he murmured.

"I love you, Kaden Galath."

His mouth took hers, intense, desperate. "I love you too, Nea. More than I can ever show you."

The hammering on the door increased. She glanced over and watched the metal bend inward.

She wished they had more time, and better options.

It was really terrible to find the man of your dreams while you were trapped by your enemy.

"We can't let them take us," she said.

The Gek'Dragar would torture them, kill them, then pull them apart for their implants. They'd do everything they could to get their hands on Oronis secrets.

Kaden closed his eyes and pressed his forehead to hers. Then he took her hand and gripped it tightly.

"You still can't use your implants?" she asked.

He shook his head. She saw his frustration and despair.

"For Oronis," she said. "For the knightqueen."

"And for us."

They stepped up to the bars.

The door burst open behind them. Nea threw an energy ball behind her.

They squeezed through the bars—Kaden first, then Nea. On the ledge outside, the wind whistled past them.

She stared down into the ravine, then she met Kaden's gaze.

They jumped.

Kaden wrapped his arms around her tightly as they fell, the wind buffeting them. They plummeted into the ravine.

A sense of calm enveloped her. She was with Kaden. The man who cherished her just as she was.

She raised her voice against the wind. "I love you, Kaden."

His face was almost savage. His mouth took hers and they kissed as they fell, embraced together.

She felt her energy charge up, filling her veins. Her eyes snapped open.

It built inside her chest, welling around her heart. Then it flowed into him.

His body jerked, his eyes glowed bright blue.

"Kaden!"

His arms locked around her. Then the world turned into a red blur.

They suddenly hit the ground—Kaden first, Nea falling on top of him.

She heard him groan, and she grimaced, her ribs sizzling with pain. She lifted her head.

They weren't smashed to pieces on the bottom of the ravine. They were in the middle of the ruined village.

She scrambled up. They weren't dead.

"*Kaden.*" She smiled. "You teleported us."

He grabbed her arms and kissed her. "You fed me energy. I felt like I was supercharged, and my oralite activated."

She didn't know what had happened, or how it had happened, but she laughed. Whatever it was, she was grateful.

They hurried over to the edge. The front of the base was crawling with Gek'Dragar. The prison's peak was heavily damaged.

But it wasn't enough. She knew they would still bring other prisoners here one day. She scowled. "We need to destroy the prison."

A look crossed Kaden's face.

She tilted her head. "You can do it, can't you?"

He looked out across the ravine. "I'm Galatine."

"Your power's stronger."

He gave a jerky nod.

"You're afraid of it."

"I had extra training to control it, harness it." He looked back at her. "But I knew it was there, a deep well of it. It's why I was mean to you at the Academy."

She sucked in a breath. "To protect me."

"Just looking at you, I felt things. It made me question my control. I never, ever wanted to hurt you or taint you."

She gripped his hands. "You *never* could. You're mine, Kaden. I trust you. I believe in you." She stepped closer and pressed a palm to his chest over his heart. "I love you. I think you can do anything." She smiled. "But don't let it go to your head, Galath."

He smiled back.

"Now, destroy that prison," she said.

His face moved into serious lines. "The remaining prisoners are still in there."

"You read the prison manifest. They've been tortured, and won't survive." She paused. "Let's free them the only way we can, and make sure no one is ever trapped here again."

Kaden lifted his hand and pointed at the prison.

Then she saw the veins in his arms glowing bright red. His brow creased as he concentrated.

A small shot of red-white light came from his hand. It pulsed straight to the top of the prison.

She frowned. It didn't look very big.

Boom.

The blast knocked them back a step. The top of the mountain exploded outward in a massive blast.

Kaden pulled her under his arm. She watched the top of the mountain crumble. Below near the bridge, Gek'-Dragar were running for their lives.

This time, it was Nea who raised her hand. She saw Gek'Dragar sprinting onto the bridge to escape the destruction.

Her energy blast hit the center of the bridge.

The two broken pieces of the bridge fell apart. She saw bodies dropping into the ravine.

She leaned into Kaden.

It was done. The prison was destroyed.

"The knightqueen and Sten?" she said.

"We'll find them. We know they're free, and they'll be searching for a way home." He touched her hair. "You need medical attention."

"So do you."

He gently squeezed her closer. "Whatever you need, I'll do it."

"Let's get back to the *Helios*. It'll be easier to scan for Carys and Sten from there. We'll find them."

He pressed a kiss to her dusty hair. "Together."

"Yes, because you're stuck with me now, Galath."

His smile was beautiful.

"WHAT DO you mean there's no sign of them?" Kaden kicked the base of the console on the bridge of the *Helios*, his frustration spilling over.

Ensign Noth shot him an apologetic look. "The nano-fluid makes it hard for the scans to pick up anything. The ground is saturated with it. I sent more probes down hoping to catch sight of the knightqueen and her guard." He shrugged. "I'm sorry. There's nothing."

Kaden fisted his hands.

Carys and Sten were out there. Hurt, in dangerous terrain. The Gek'Dragar would be hunting for them. He'd failed them.

A hand ran down his back, and it felt like a cool breeze on his face. He leaned into Nea's touch.

"What Kaden means is thank you, Ensign." She turned to him. "Don't undo all the healing the captain did on you."

When he'd first returned to the *Helios*, the first thing Kaden had done was pass out. The final teleport and his injuries had burned him out.

Thankfully, Nea had gotten the crew searching for Carys and Sten. Kaden had woken up in sick bay with Captain Attaway running the medical equipment on him. His oralite was functioning again, but he had a splitting headache, and still-healing wounds.

He'd stood over the captain while she'd treated Nea, until he was satisfied that she was no longer bleeding internally. He knew her ribs were still tender.

"Can we deduce where the queen and her guard might go?" the ensign asked.

Kaden shook his head. "No, Knightguard Sten will do what's least expected in order to avoid the Gek'Dragar. He was raised to protect the knightqueen, and has spent over a decade doing it. He's good. Really good. He'd die for her. He'll do whatever is required to keep her alive."

"They'll turn up," Nea said. "We keep looking. We'll stay close by, under camouflage."

Kaden scowled at the viewscreen. "The Gek'Dragar will likely send reinforcements."

"If they do, we'll deal with it. Like you said, Sten will keep Carys safe. And our queen is not defenseless. They're free, that's the most important thing."

He snaked an arm around her and pulled her close. He pressed his forehead to hers, then kissed her.

"Well, I see one good thing has come out of all of this."

At the captain's remark, Nea looked over.

"Yes, the knighthunter has grown on me," Nea said. "I've decided he isn't quite as annoying as I'd first thought."

Chief Watson snorted. "And the boy is easy on the eyes too."

"Thank you, Chief," Kaden said.

"But you'll have to keep him out of trouble," the chief added.

"I'll try," Nea said with a smile.

The chief snorted. "Or you'll just join in."

Nea's smile widened.

That smile made every hard thing Kaden had ever endured worth it. She loved him. For the first time in his life, he was the most important person to someone.

He lowered his voice. "So, you love me?"

Her eyelids lowered. "Yes."

"Nea, I don't know anything about love."

"I'm not an expert, either." She threaded her fingers

through his. "But I'm very good at studying and learning. And I always try to be the best at what I do."

His lips quirked. "Oh, I know."

"So, I think together, we'll work it out." She pressed her hands to his chest. "And do it very well."

He couldn't help but kiss her again.

"All right, you two," Chief Watson grumbled. "Get out of here. You're giving me a hot flash."

She sounded grumpy, but the woman was smiling.

"Go and rest," Captain Attaway said with a smile. "If our scans detect any sign of the knightqueen, we'll let you know immediately."

With a murmur of thanks, Kaden led Nea off the bridge.

Their mission hadn't ended the way he'd hoped, but he couldn't help but feel like he'd won anyway.

With Nea by his side, he'd always feel that way.

"Shall we go and get some rest, Galath?"

"Well, we'll be in bed." He slid his hand down to her ass. "But I'm not planning on sleeping."

"I think we're in agreement."

"First time for everything." When she pinched his side, he laughed.

Yes, he'd definitely won.

CHAPTER TWENTY

K aden felt Nea move away from him in the bed, and tightened his hold on her.

He heard a low chuckle, then she pressed a kiss to the underside of his jaw. "I need the washroom." Her voice was still husky from sleep. "I'll be right back."

He relaxed his arms, and she slipped away. He opened his eyes and watched her walk across the cabin, naked.

He smiled.

His. She was his.

Nothing in his life had ever truly belonged just to him.

He noted the fading scrapes and bruises on her skin. He remembered how hurt she'd been. He wouldn't let it happen again. She was his to love, his to protect.

When she returned, her hair was brushed to a shiny, black sleekness. She sat down beside him on the bed, and he shifted, wrapping an arm around her hip, and pressing his face to her stomach. He nuzzled her.

Her hands stroked his hair, her fingers massaging his scalp. He pushed into her touch.

"Ah, the fierce knighthunter likes to be petted." She played with his hair some more. "I know you're awake, Kaden."

He made a sound. "I only like to be petted by you."

Now she tugged on his hair. "Good. How's your oralite?"

"Everything is functioning at one hundred percent capacity." He rolled, pushing her onto her back in the center of the bed. He kept going until he was on top of her.

"Careful, you're still healing," she admonished. "I seem to recall you fainting on the bridge."

"I didn't faint."

She looked like she was trying not to laugh. "Sure."

"I'm fine." He slid a hand between her legs, touching her possessively.

She let out a sexy humming sound.

"Let me show you how fine I feel," he murmured. "I'm feeling the need to prove myself."

"No, I'll show you, Knighthunter." She pushed at his chest. "Roll onto your back."

Kaden obeyed. When she straddled him, he couldn't look away. He let his gaze drift over her, a part of him wanting to make sure she wasn't injured anywhere else. He cupped one of her breasts. "I can't believe that you're mine."

She leaned down and nipped his lips. "Believe it. Now, are you going to be good?"

"I'm never usually good."

She gave him a feminine smile that made his gut clench.

"You will be if you want me to suck your cock."

The organ in question twitched, and her smile widened.

"Good, Knighthunter." She pressed her body to his, peppering kisses across his chest.

He slid his hand into his woman's hair. She owned him, body and soul. There was nothing he wouldn't do for her.

"I'm only good for you," he said.

She scraped her teeth across his ribs, moving lower. "I'm happy to hear that."

TWO HOURS LATER, Kaden sat hunched over the work spread out on the table in front of him. He'd taken over one of the *Helios'* forward observation rooms. A bank of windows gave a perfect view of Ti-Lore.

His body was loose and relaxed. He smiled. Nea made sure he was feeling *very* good when they'd left their cabin.

She'd gone to check in with the captain, and to see about facilitating a call to Oron.

Kaden had come here to do some research. He picked up the porta-comp. It was filled with old documents on Galatine.

There were only five recorded Galatine, including himself. All of them had possessed a genetic mutation that had made them better designed to link with the oralite implant all knights were given. They were able to generate and direct energy in unique ways.

But he wanted to know what had happened when he and Nea had fallen into that ravine.

Her energy had powered him, and somehow gotten his damaged oralite working again.

He picked up the porta-comp and swiped the screen, reading the text. He wasn't sure how much time had passed, but he finally found something that might explain what happened. When he finished reading, he sat back in his chair and his gaze locked on Ti-Lore.

Where were Sten and Carys? Were they all right? Were they injured?

Kaden's lips compressed. He wanted them safe, but there was still no sign of them.

The doors opened and Nea strode in. She smiled at him.

"Hello, Knighthunter." She draped an arm across his shoulders and kissed his cheek. "You look like you're working hard."

"Any news on Carys and Sten?"

Her smile faded. "Not yet. We have to have faith and a lot of patience."

He managed a nod.

Then Nea pulled something from her pocket, and held it up. It was a tala fruit.

He met her gaze.

"Funny," she said. "I found tala fruit in the food printer on a Terran ship."

"Really?"

She nipped his ear. "It was you. You left them for me at the Academy."

He didn't look away from her blue-green gaze. "They were your favorite."

Warmth filled her gaze. "I love you." Then her gaze dropped to the porta-comp in his hands. "What are you doing?"

"Researching Galatine." He pulled her onto his lap. "I found a reference. It's from centuries ago, when a Galatine was injured on the battlefield. His forbidden lover was also a knight. Back then, any Galatine was kept separate from knights and the regular population. They were kept locked up, not allowed contact with others, and brought out and used like weapons."

"I'm glad times have changed." She played with his hair. "And I'm glad this long-ago Galatine rebelled and fell in love."

"Somehow, in the middle of a battle, this Galatine and his lover...linked. Her energy powered him, and they turned the tide of the battle." He smiled. "The language is a little flowery, but it talks of their souls being joined."

She pressed a palm to his chest. "Is your soul all mine?"

"Yes. Every part of it."

Her face softened. "Kaden."

He gripped her hand. "Nea, I..."

When he paused, she raised a brow. "What?"

He swallowed, dredging up the courage to ask the question burning on his tongue. "Will you marry me?"

Her mouth dropped open, pure shock on her face.

His chest tightened. "If you don't want to—"

"I want to." Her hands cupped his face. "Of course, I want to. You just surprised me."

Then her mouth was on his. He pulled her closer, thrusting his tongue between her lips.

"Let the girl breathe, Knighthunter." It was the amused voice of Chief Watson.

He and Nea broke apart, and when he looked over his shoulder, he saw most of the skeleton crew, led by Captain Attaway. Everyone was carrying plates and glasses.

"We decided a little celebration was in order." Ensign Noth lifted some bottles. "I know we don't have the knightqueen and her guard yet, but nor do the Gek'Dragar. That's worth celebrating."

Nea smiled. "I think that's an excellent idea. We couldn't have gotten this far without all of you. And we have something else to celebrate. Knighthunter Kaden and I are getting married."

There were shocked exclamations. The chief was shaking her head but smiling, and the captain beamed at them.

"Congratulations," Captain Attaway said. "We're very happy for both of you."

"Let's party," the chief said. "Let her go, Knighthunter. You can drag her off to your cabin later."

Kaden, a man so used to being alone, found himself surrounded by allies, friends, and the woman he loved.

"Captain, I have a favor to ask," he said.

Captain Attaway lifted her glass. "Anything."

NEA FIDGETED, and stroked her hands down her dress.

"Nea, you look beautiful."

Captain Attaway stepped up behind her. Nea stood in front of the mirror. She wore a column of gold with tiny straps. The silky fabric slicked over her body. Her hair was loose, and her lips were red.

She did look beautiful.

She'd never imagined getting married. She'd never met a man who tempted her to consider it, and she'd never been in love. Work had always been her focus.

She smiled. Clearly, she'd been waiting for one man. One that just a short time ago, she would never, ever have believed she'd be in love with.

"Here," the captain said. "It's a tradition on Earth to have a bouquet of flowers at your wedding."

The small bunch was made up of beautiful white flowers.

"Thank you." Nea took them. "And thank you for doing this."

The captain smiled. "When Kaden asked me to officiate the ceremony, I was thrilled. It's not often I get to marry anyone. Are you ready?"

She nodded. She was. She felt a deep sense of certainty in her chest.

She walked with the captain to the bridge of the *Helios*. The doors opened, and all the skeleton crew were there, but all she could see was Kaden.

He stood tall and straight, clad in fitted black pants and a doublet-style shirt. His face was cool and blank, but she knew him well enough now to know that he was hiding what he felt.

Until he looked at her. Then she saw the love blazing in his eyes.

She walked with the captain toward him. When she reached him, he took her hand.

"You look beautiful," he murmured.

"Thank you." She pressed a hand to his cheek. "You look handsome and dangerous." She lowered her voice. "My favorite combination."

"We are gathered here today to share the union of two people who are very much in love," Captain Attaway said. "Two people who've made duty and honor the cornerstone of their lives. And today, they also pledged their lives to each other." The captain smiled at them. "Knightmaster Nea Laurier and Knighthunter Kaden Galath."

Nea stared into Kaden's glittering blue eyes and listened to the captain's words about love and commitment. That sense of rightness and love swelled inside her.

"The groom has something for the bride," the captain said.

Kaden cleared his throat. "It's a Terran tradition, so I'm told, to give your wife a ring. A symbol of love, commitment, and a sacred bond." He held up a silver ring that was covered in a glitter of stones in brilliant-white and aqua-blue.

"It's beautiful," Nea murmured.

He slid the ring onto her finger on her left hand.

"It seemed fitting since the Terrans helped bring us together," he said.

"I'm still half surprised you two didn't kill each other," Chief Watson muttered.

Light laughter moved through the crowd.

"I need to get you a ring," Nea told him.

"I'll wear it with pride."

"And with that," Captain Attaway said. "You may now kiss your bride."

Cheers and clapping erupted, and Nea smiled as Kaden pulled her into his arms. He kissed her like there was no one else in the room. Like he needed the kiss to survive.

"Phew, hot flash," the chief murmured.

"And now we get to have another party," Ensign Noth said.

Suddenly, a console beeped. Everyone turned from happy guests to alert crew in an instant.

Ensign Noth hurried to the console, swiping and tapping.

"Ensign?" the captain said.

"A probe on the planet's surface detected something."

Nea clutched Kaden's hand.

"It picked something up north of the Gek'Dragar prison location. Deep into the mountains, down in one of the ravines."

A blurry image appeared on viewscreen. It was in the base of a ravine, the darkness making it hard to see anything. Nea made out a jumble of rocks.

Then she saw movement.

A woman climbed over the rocks, and a second later, a much larger man came into view.

The woman turned her head, scanning the ravine, then the pair disappeared deeper into the ravine.

The ensign zoomed in on a still shot of the couple. Nea's heart beat hard.

It was Carys. She was dirty, with a scrape on her cheek and her hair tangled, but it was the knightqueen. And Sten was with her.

"They're alive," Nea said.

"Where are they?" Kaden barked. "Can we get to them?"

Ensign Noth winced. "Um, no. About thirty seconds after this, something destroyed the probe. I'm guessing they took it out. We've lost them."

Kaden cursed.

Nea pressed a hand to her husband's arm. That gave her thrill. *Her husband.* "Sten and Carys have no idea that the probes are ours," she said. "They're not an Oronis design, and the probably think that they're Gek'Dragar."

Kaden ran a hand through his hair.

"I've sent another probe to the area to keep searching," Ensign Noth said.

"Thank you, Ensign," the captain replied.

"They're alive," Nea said. "That's the most important thing. There's nothing more we can do right now except wait."

"Nea's right," Chief Watson said. "But we do have a marriage to celebrate. Time to break out the whiskey."

CHAPTER TWENTY-ONE

"We have visual confirmation, Ashtin. They are alive."

On the screen in Captain Attaway's office, Nea watched Knightmaster Ashtin Caydor blow out a breath.

"That's good news, Nea."

"We won't stop until we find them and bring them home."

He nodded. "I know. I never doubted you or Kaden. I know the two of you don't get along, but both of you are the best knights I have."

Oh. She probably needed to share with him that things had changed.

"You sent more probes down to the planet?" Ashtin asked.

"Yes. We'll keep searching." It was so frustrating that they hadn't gotten another glimpse of the pair.

"And the Gek'Dragar?"

Nea sighed. "A warship arrived an hour ago. They've sent more troops to scour the surface."

Ashtin cursed.

"I *know* that Sten and Carys can elude them. They'll get out." She paused. "How are things on Oron?"

"Our people are understandably concerned. I'd love to be able to share this sighting of Carys and Sten, but it would put their lives at risk. I'm doing my best to reassure everyone that our queen is alive, and we're doing everything we can to bring her home." His handsome face softened. "Luckily, my new Space Corps liaison from Earth is a good distraction for everyone. Kennedy sort of charms everyone everywhere she goes. She's been busy learning everything she can about Oron."

"Love looks good on you, Knightmaster."

Ashtin's smile widened. "You should try it."

"Oh, well." Nea felt heat in her cheeks.

"Is that the *Helios*?" Kennedy appeared on screen, a wide smile on her face. Her small, ball-shaped drone, Beep, buzzed around her head.

Kennedy looked exactly how Nea imagined a smart, energetic Space Corps officer should look. She had a friendly, open face, and brown hair in a long braid. She touched Ashtin's arm, the link between the pair obvious.

"Is everybody okay?" Kennedy asked.

"Hi, Kennedy," Nea said. "Everyone aboard is fine."

"I'm *so* glad you're okay, Nea. Ashtin's told me that it's been a grueling mission."

Nea tucked a strand of hair behind her ear. "Thanks."

Kennedy's gaze latched onto Nea's ring. "That's a beautiful ring. You know, on Earth, people wear a ring on that finger of their left hand when they've gotten married."

"Really?" Nea said.

The xenoanthropologist's face lit up. "Yes. It's a tradition that started in—"

Ashtin wrapped an arm around Kennedy's waist. "I don't think Nea is married." He laughed.

Nea leaned forward and took a deep breath. "Actually..."

Ashtin and Kennedy went silent, staring at her.

"Surprise," Nea said sheepishly.

"You got *married*?" Ashtin said. "In the middle of a dangerous mission in Gek'Dragar space?" He was enunciating the words like he couldn't quite believe what he was saying.

Nea cocked a brow. "Didn't you and Kennedy fall in love in the middle of a dangerous mission?"

Kennedy laughed. "She's got you there, Knightmaster."

A dull flush ran along Ashtin's cheeks.

"So you fell for a member of the *Helios* crew?" Kennedy asked. "Who?"

The office door opened and Kaden strode in. He stopped beside her, then slid a hand under her hair and squeezed the back of her neck.

"Ashtin," he said. "Good to see you, Kennedy."

The pair were both still staring.

"So," Nea said. "Kaden and I—"

"Got married?" Ashtin blinked. "You're playing a joke on me, right?"

Kaden tipped Nea's face up, then pressed a kiss to her lips. "No."

The way he looked at her made her shiver.

"Oh my God." Kennedy laughed. "This is *so* great. No one saw this coming."

Kaden sat down beside Nea and took her hand.

Ashtin was still staring, his gaze moving from one of them to the other. "I guess I shouldn't be too shocked, since he had a thing for you at the Academy."

"He was horrible to me at the Academy," Nea said.

Kaden pulled her closer. "But she's forgiven me."

"Mostly..."

Kennedy laughed again. "I'm pretty sure Ashtin would be less shocked if you'd killed each other."

Nea smiled at the Terran woman. "We fell in love instead."

Ashtin shook his head and let out a laugh. "Well, I'm happy for you both. We'll have to celebrate when you get home to Oron." Then he cleared his throat. "Ah, Nea. Your father is waiting to talk to you. He pulled some strings so he could use part of this transmission." Ashtin didn't look pleased about it.

She rolled her eyes. Of course, her father had to force his way in.

"All right, thanks, Ashtin."

"Well done to both of you. It's been a difficult mission, but destroying the Gek'Dragar prison was an excellent outcome. And I know that the knightqueen and Sten will be back safe on Oron soon."

Kaden nodded.

The screen went black, with the seal of the Knight-force in the center.

"I'd better talk to my father alone," she said.

"No. I'm not leaving you alone with him." Kaden rose and stepped to the side. "I'll stay out of view, but if he says one *gul*-vexed thing to you—"

She reached out and grabbed his hand. "He can't hurt me anymore. The love and acceptance I've always wanted, you give me that."

"I love you, Nea." He sucked in a breath. "If you want to keep our marriage a secret for now, I understand."

She opened her mouth to reply, but the screen changed. Kaden stepped back out of view.

Her father appeared on the screen. He looked as regal as always, but there was a fierce scowl on his face.

"Hello, Father."

"Your mission is a failure, Nea. How could you not have found and secured the knightqueen by now?"

She saw Kaden stiffen, but held up a hand to him.

"I'm fine, Father. Thanks for asking. My injuries are healing. And yes, we managed to track down the knightqueen through Gek'Dragar space, and she is at least free of our enemies. I have no doubt we'll find her and her knightguard soon."

"Sarcasm is crass, Nea." Her father gave a dismissive wave. "People know you're heading this mission. It's a disgrace to the Laurier name that you haven't—"

Kaden's face looked carved from stone, but a muscle ticked in his jaw. She suspected he was ready to blow.

To her, her father's words were barely a sting. She realized now that she didn't want or need his approval. She knew she was an excellent knightmaster. She knew who she was, and now she had a man who showed her daily how much he admired her. How much he cared for her.

"I don't care about the Laurier name," she said. "I care about being a good knight, doing what's right and helping others, having integrity."

Her father's face turned even more fierce, and he opened his mouth.

That's when Kaden stepped into view. "Weigh your next words carefully, Laurier. I won't have you insult her."

Nea fought back a smile.

Her father's gaze narrowed on Kaden. "You."

"I'm not heading this mission, Father," Nea continued. "Kaden and I are equal partners."

"Then I suppose his incompetence is to blame—"

"*Quiet*," Nea snapped.

Her father looked shocked. She'd never spoken to him like that before.

"Kaden is an excellent knighthunter. The best. And you know that. I'd be dead if it wasn't for him."

Kaden's lips twitched. "I can say the same to you."

She took his hand and squeezed it.

Her father's face turned red, and he stared at their joined hands.

She lifted her chin. "Father, I won't listen to you speak badly of me, or my husband."

Her father's eyes bulged. "Husband?" He choked out the word.

"Yes, Captain Attaway married Kaden and me. I love him. He's one of the best men I've ever met."

Kaden leaned down and kissed her. "I love you."

"This is outrageous—"

"Enough." Nea rose, and Kaden slid an arm around her. "I'm not an elitist snob like you are, Father. I don't believe I'm better than others because of my name. Kaden is a hundred times the man you are. We'll see you when we're back on Oron, *if* you can be civil. And we will return with the knightqueen, have no doubt about that." She ended the call.

"Feel good?" Kaden asked.

She nodded. "It does. He's my father, and he isn't always insufferable, but he doesn't dictate my life or my happiness."

Kaden pulled her closer. "Your happiness is my job now, my wife."

Oh, *wife*. She was going to have to get used to that. "How are you going to make me happy, my husband?"

He lowered his head. "Let me show you."

CARYS CLIMBED OVER THE ROCKS, wincing as she added more cuts to her feet. The wrappings Sten had put on them had fallen off long ago. The soles of her feet were bloody and raw.

What she'd give for a pair of boots right now.

Her combat implant was blocking most of the pain, but after days of captivity, she couldn't quite block all her tiredness, hunger, and soreness.

Not that she was going to complain. One, because she was the Knightqueen of Oronis. She'd fight to survive to her dying breath.

Her people were depending on her. She would not fail the Oronis.

On her next step, she winced again. Mostly, she wouldn't complain because otherwise, her hardheaded, overprotective knightguard would carry her.

She glanced at Sten as he vaulted over some rocks. Big, solid, secure Sten. He'd given her a sense of safety and security for over a decade. Especially when her parents had been assassinated.

She had been seventeen the first time she'd seen him. She remembered her heart thudding hard. He'd been bigger and broader than any Oronis, with a rugged face. Solid like an immovable mountain.

At first, she'd been certain he never smiled or laughed. But she'd slowly gotten him to open up to her.

"Stop," his deep voice rumbled. His big hand cupped her shoulder.

She saw his gaze was on her bleeding feet.

"I'm fine, Sten. I can keep going."

"Sit."

She rolled her eyes. She knew better than to argue.

She perched on a rock. Her once grand ballgown was now just dirty tatters. The ball on Oron felt so long ago, even though she knew it had only been days since the Gek'Dragar had abducted her right out of her palace. Anger was a tumultuous simmer inside her.

Sten's quick thinking of joining them with a dura-

binding around their wrists meant she wasn't alone. It couldn't be removed without killing them both.

The Gek'Dragar had punished him for it.

The binding was still linking them. While they were being hunted by the Gek'Dragar, he refused to remove it. The glowing cord rested between them.

As he knelt beside her, she looked upward.

They were in the bottom of a huge chasm. It was the deepest she'd ever seen. Jagged cliff faces rose up on either side, and down here it was dark and gloomy. She caught a glimpse of the blue sky, far, far overhead.

A distant, throaty roar echoed through the canyon, and she shivered. There were all kinds of horrible beasts down here. They'd seen some, but had successfully avoided them.

So far.

Carys knew the Gek'Dragar would be coming, hunting them. She'd already destroyed one probe that had tried to track them.

Sten studied her feet, a fierce scowl on his face.

He gripped the bottom of his already torn shirt, and ripped off a strip of fabric. He gently wrapped it around one of her bare feet. He ripped another strip, and wrapped her other foot. Carys closed her eyes and enjoyed the feel of his strong hands.

If the man knew just how much she wanted him to touch her, and where, he'd be shocked and horrified.

Unfortunately for her, dependable and noble knight-guard Thorsten Carahan, still saw her as a teenager, and as his untouchable queen.

"There." He set her foot down, his green gaze on her face.

Most Oronis had black hair or platinum-blonde hair like hers. Sten's was brown, and he kept it cut very short. He wasn't lean like most Oronis either. His body was broader and more muscular. He had a scar on one cheek, and he'd never had it removed. He'd gotten it protecting her from a vicious animal when she was eighteen. It had been during the same attack that had killed her parents. She'd been terrified and grieving, but Sten had kept her safe for days.

And now he was keeping her safe again.

Her job was to ensure that he didn't get killed in the process, because she had no doubt he'd die for her.

And she wasn't going to let that happen.

He pulled a small bottle off his belt. He'd managed to snag it from the prison. "Drink."

She took a sip of the water, feeling it wet her parched throat. She'd noted that he'd barely had any of the water. "Now you." She held it out to him.

"I'm fine."

"Sten, that's an order."

His grumpy look had her hiding a smile. But the urge to smile didn't last long. One side of his face was covered in terrible bruises, with swelling around his eye. She knew his implants would be healing it, but the Gek'-Dragar had beaten him severely. They'd made her watch.

The memory had her stomach doing a sickening roll, and the water threatened to come back up.

"Carys?"

She looked up and pasted on a smile. She reached out and touched his bruises. "Are these all right?"

He nodded.

"I need..."

"What?" He leaned closer. "Anything?"

"A hug."

He stiffened, and she thought he'd refuse, but just when she'd given up hope, he pulled her into his arms.

She settled against his broad chest with a sigh. The man gave off so much heat. His brawny arms closed around her. She closed her eyes, and for a second, imagined they were in her rooms at the Castle Aravena. Alone, in front of a roaring fireplace.

"I promise I'll keep you safe." His deep voice surrounded her. "I promise I'll get you home."

She pressed a hand to his chest, over the solid thud of his heart. "*We'll* get home."

Suddenly, there was a sound. Rocks scraping against rocks.

Sten shot to his feet and set her beside him.

They both scanned the gloom. Carys didn't see or sense anything.

The beast charged out of nowhere.

It aimed straight at Sten, tackling him to the rocky ground.

Carys got the impression of a gray-furred body, and overlong, powerful arms. Some creature, built for climbing, had been mutated by what the Gek'Dragar had done to this planet.

Sten rolled, his face contorted, and his hands pressed

to the creature's chest. He was trying to keep the fang-filled mouth from clamping onto his head.

Carys formed her sword, energy flowing through her.

The blade glowed blue in the shadows.

The creature lifted its head, realizing another danger was nearby.

Carys leaped forward, swinging her sword. With one slash, the creature's head left its body and hit the ground.

Sten jumped to his feet. There were three new claw slashes across his chest. He formed his own sword—a huge broadsword twice the size of hers.

Three more beasts, the same as the first, loped over the rocks and charged toward them.

Carys let her anger fuel her. Anger at her abduction, at Sten's beatings, fury at the Gek'Dragar.

She swung her sword, cutting at the beast.

She and Sten worked together, lunging and swinging. He was pure, unstoppable power. She gathered a ball of energy on her palm and tossed it. The beast let out a deafening yowl.

With a roar, Sten wielded his sword, slashing down another beast.

Finally, the beasts were all dead.

Carys lowered her sword, her chest heaving.

Sten's sword dissolved away, his gaze never leaving the shadows as he searched for more dangers.

"We need to go," he said. "We need to get far away from here."

Yes. The Gek'Dragar would take one look at these dead beasts and know it was them.

Her sword retracted, and she nodded.

Sten grabbed her hand. "With my blood and body, I will be your shield and sword. I will keep you safe."

She squeezed his fingers. "I know, Sten. But we're in this together." She was the knightqueen and people sometimes forgot that she was a knight as well. Especially her hard-headed knightguard. "Lead the way. Let's find a way home."

I hope you enjoyed Nea and Kaden's story!

Oronis Knights continues with *Knightqueen*, starring Knightqueen Carys and Knightguard Sten. Coming early 2024.

Want to find out more about the Eon Warriors? Check out the first book in the **Eon Warriors**, *Edge of Eon*. **Read on for a preview of the first chapter.**

Don't miss out! For updates about new releases, free books, and other fun stuff, sign up for my VIP mailing list and get your *free box set* containing three action-packed romances.

Visit here to get started: www.annahackett.com

Would you like a FREE BOX SET of my books?

PREVIEW: EDGE OF EON

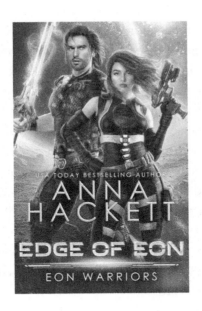

She shifted on the chair, causing the chains binding her hands to clank together. Eve Traynor snorted. The wrist and ankle restraints were overkill. She was on a low-orbit prison circling Earth. Where the fuck did they think she was going to go?

Eve shifted her shoulders to try to ease the tension from having her hands tied behind her back. For the millionth time, she studied her surroundings. The medium-sized room was empty, except for her chair. Everything from the floor to the ceiling was dull-gray metal. All of the Citadel Prison was drab and sparse. She'd learned every boring inch of it the last few months.

One wide window provided the only break in the otherwise uniform space. Outside, she caught a tantalizing glimpse of the blue-green orb of Earth below.

Her gut clenched and she drank in the sight of her home. Five months she'd been locked away in this prison. Five months since her life had imploded.

She automatically thought of her sisters. She sucked in a deep breath. She hated everything they'd had to go through because of what had happened. Hell, she thought of her mom as well, even though their last contact had been the day after Eve had been imprisoned. Her mom had left Eve a drunken, scathing message.

The door to the room opened, and Eve lifted her chin and braced.

When she saw the dark-blue Space Corps uniform, she stiffened. When she saw the row of stars on the lapel, she gritted her teeth.

Admiral Linda Barber stepped into the room, accompanied by a female prison guard. The admiral's hair was its usual sleek bob of highlighted, ash-blonde hair. Her brown eyes were steady.

Eve looked at the guard. "Take me back to my cell."

The admiral lifted a hand. "Please leave us."

The guard hesitated. "That's against protocol, ma'am—"

"It'll be fine." The admiral's stern voice said she was giving an order, not making a request.

The guard hesitated again, then ducked through the door. It clicked closed behind her.

Eve sniffed. "Say what you have to say and leave."

Admiral Barber sighed, taking a few steps closer. "I know you're angry. You have a right to be—"

"You think?" Eve sucked back the rush of molten anger. "I got tossed under the fucking starship to save a mama's boy. A mama's boy who had no right to be in command of one of Space Corps' vessels."

Shit. Eve wanted to pummel something. Preferably the face of Robert J. Hathaway—golden son of Rear-Admiral Elisabeth Hathaway. A man who, because of family connections, was given captaincy of the *Orion*, even though he lacked the intelligence and experience needed to lead it.

Meanwhile, Eve—a Space Corps veteran—had worked her ass off during her career in the Corps, and had been promised her own ship, only to be denied her chance. Instead, she'd been assigned as Hathaway's second-in-command. To be a glorified babysitter, and to actually run the ship, just without the title and the pay raise.

She'd swallowed it. Swallowed Hathaway's incompetence and blowhard bullshit. Until he'd fucked up. Big-time.

"The Haumea Incident was regrettable," Barber said.

Eve snorted. "Mostly for the people who died. And definitely for me, since I'm the one shackled to a chair in the Citadel. Meanwhile, I assume Bobby Hathaway is still a dedicated Space Corps employee."

"He's no longer a captain of a ship. And he never will be again."

"Right. Mommy got him a cushy desk job back at Space Corps Headquarters."

The silence was deafening and it made Eve want to kick something.

"I'm sorry, Eve. We all know what happened wasn't right."

Eve jerked on her chains and they clanked against the chair. "And you let it happen. All of Space Corps leadership did, to appease Mommy Hathaway. I dedicated my life to the Corps, and you all screwed me over for an admiral's incompetent son. I got sentenced to prison for *his* mistakes." Stomach turning in vicious circles, Eve looked at the floor, sucking in air. She stared at the soft booties on her feet. Damned inmate footwear. She wasn't even allowed proper fucking shoes.

Admiral Barber moved to her side. "I'm here to offer you a chance at freedom."

Gaze narrowing, Eve looked up. Barber looked... nervous. Eve had never seen the self-assured woman nervous before.

"There's a mission. If you complete it, you'll be released from prison."

Interesting. "And reinstated? With a full pardon?"

Barber's lips pursed and her face looked pinched. "We can negotiate."

So, no. "Screw your offer." Eve would prefer to rot in her cell, rather than help the Space Corps.

The admiral moved in front of her, her low-heeled pumps echoing on the floor. "Eve, the fate of the world depends on this mission."

Barber's serious tone sent a shiver skating down Eve's spine. She met the woman's brown eyes.

"The Kantos are gathering their forces just beyond the boundary at Station Omega V."

Fuck. The Kantos. The insectoid alien race had been nipping at Earth for years. Their humanoid-insectoid soldiers were the brains of the operation, but they encompassed all manner of ugly, insect-like beasts as well.

With the invention of zero-point drives several decades ago, Earth's abilities for space exploration had exploded. Then, thirty years ago, they'd made first contact with an alien species—the Eon.

The Eon shared a common ancestor with the humans of Earth. They were bigger and broader, with a few differing organs, but generally human-looking. They had larger lungs, a stronger, bigger heart, and a more efficiently-designed digestion system. This gave them increased strength and stamina, which in turn made them excellent warriors. Unfortunately, they also wanted nothing to do with Earth and its inferior Terrans.

The Eon, and their fearsome warriors and warships, stayed inside their own space and had banned Terrans from crossing their boundaries.

Then, twenty years ago, the first unfortunate and bloody meeting with the Kantos had occurred.

Since then, the Kantos had returned repeatedly to

nip at the Terran borders—attacking ships, space stations, and colonies.

But it had become obvious in the last year or so that the Kantos had something bigger planned. The Haumea Incident had made that crystal clear.

The Kantos wanted Earth. There were to be no treaties, alliances, or negotiations. They wanted to descend like locusts and decimate everything—all the planet's resources, and most of all, the humans.

Yes, the Kantos wanted to freaking use humans as a food source. Eve suppressed a shudder.

"And?" she said.

"We have to do whatever it takes to save our planet."

Eve tilted her head. "The Eon."

Admiral Barber smiled. "You were always sharp, Eve. Yes, the Eon are the only ones with the numbers, the technology, and the capability to help us repel the Kantos."

"Except they want nothing to do with us." No one had seen or spoken with an Eon for three decades.

"Desperate times call for desperate measures."

Okay, Eve felt that shiver again. She felt like she was standing on the edge of a platform, about to be shoved under the starship again.

"What's the mission?" she asked carefully.

"We want you to abduct War Commander Davion Thann-Eon."

Holy fuck. Eve's chest clenched so tight she couldn't even draw a breath. Then the air rushed into her lungs, and she threw her head back and laughed. Tears ran down her face.

"You're kidding."

But the admiral wasn't laughing.

Eve shook her head. "That's a fucking suicide mission. You want me to abduct the deadliest, most decorated Eon war commander who controls the largest, most destructive Eon warship in their fleet?"

"Yes."

"No."

"Eve, you have a record of making...risky decisions."

Eve shook her head. "I always calculate the risks."

"Yes, but you use a higher margin of error than the rest of us."

"I've always completed my missions successfully." The Haumea Incident excluded, since that was Bobby's brilliant screw-up.

"Yes. That's why we know if anyone has a chance of making this mission a success, it's you."

"I may as well take out a blaster and shoot myself right now. One, I'll never make it into Eon space, let alone aboard the *Desteron*."

Since the initial encounter, they'd collected whatever intel they could on the Eon. Eve had seen secret schematics of that warship. And she had to admit, the thought of being aboard that ship left her a little damp between her thighs. She loved space and flying, and the big, sleek warship was something straight out of her fantasies.

"We have an experimental, top-of-the-line stealth ship for you to use," the admiral said.

Eve carried on like the woman hadn't spoken. "And two, even if I got close to the war commander, he's bigger and stronger than me, not to mention bonded to a fucking deadly alien symbiont that gives him added strength and the ability to create organic armor and weapons with a single thought. I'd be dead in seconds."

"We recovered a...substance that is able to contain the symbiont the Eon use."

Eve narrowed her eyes. "Recovered from where?"

Admiral Barber cleared her throat. "From the wreck of a Kantos ship. It was clearly tech they were developing to use against the Eon."

Shit. "So I'm to abduct the war commander, and then further enrage him by neutralizing his symbiont."

"We believe the containment is temporary, and there is an antidote."

Eve shook her head. "This is beyond insane."

"For the fate of humanity, we have to try."

"*Talk* to them," Eve said. "Use some diplomacy."

"We tried. They refused all contact."

Because humans were simply ants to the Eon. Small, insignificant, an annoyance.

Although, truth be told, humanity only had itself to blame. By all accounts, Terrans hadn't behaved very well at first contact. The meetings with the Eon had turned into blustering threats, different countries trying to make alliances with the aliens while happily stabbing each other in the back.

Now Earth wanted to abduct an Eon war commander. No, not a war commander, *the* war commander. So dumb. She wished she had a hand free so she could slap it over her eyes.

"Find another sacrificial lamb."

The admiral was silent for a long moment. "If you won't do it for yourself or for humanity, then do it for your sisters."

Eve's blood chilled and she cocked her head. "What's this got to do with my sisters?"

"They've made a lot of noise about your imprisonment. Agitating for your freedom."

Eve breathed through her nose. God, she loved her sisters. Still, she didn't know whether to be pleased or pissed. "And?"

"Your sister has shared some classified information with the press about the Haumea Incident."

Eve fought back a laugh. Lara wasn't shy about sharing her thoughts about this entire screwed-up situation. Eve's older sister was a badass Space Corps special forces marine. Lara wouldn't hesitate to take down anyone who pissed her off, the Space Corps included.

"And she had access to information she should not have had access to, meaning your other sister has done some...creative hacking."

Dammit. The rush of love was mixed with some annoyance. Sweet, geeky Wren had a giant, super-smart brain. She was a computer-systems engineer for some company with cutting-edge technology in Japan. It helped keep her baby sister's big brain busy, because Wren hadn't found a computer she couldn't hack.

"Plenty of people are unhappy with what your sisters have been stirring up," Barber continued.

Eve stiffened. She didn't like where this was going.

"I've tried to run interference—"

"Admiral—"

Barber held up a hand. "I can't keep protecting them, Eve. I've been trying, but some of this is even above my pay grade. If you don't do this mission, powers outside of my control will go after them. They'll both end up in a cell right alongside yours until the Kantos arrive and blow this prison out of the sky."

Her jaw tight, Eve's brain turned all the information over. *Fucking fuck.*

"Eve, if there is anyone who has a chance of succeeding on this mission, it's you."

Eve stayed silent.

Barber stepped closer. "I don't care if you do it for yourself, the billions of people of Earth, or your sisters—"

"I'll do it." The words shot out of Eve, harsh and angry.

She'd do it—abduct the scariest alien war commander in the galaxy—for all the reasons the admiral listed—to clear her name, for her freedom, to save the world, and for the sisters she loved.

Honestly, it didn't matter anyway, because the odds of her succeeding and coming back alive were zero.

EVE LEFT THE STARSHIP GYM, towel around her neck, and her muscles warm and limber from her workout.

God, it was nice to work out when it suited her. On the Citadel Prison, exercise time was strictly scheduled, monitored, and timed.

Two crew members came into view, heading down

the hall toward her. As soon as the uniformed men spotted her, they looked at the floor and passed her quickly.

Eve rolled her eyes. Well, she wasn't aboard the *Polaris* to make friends, and she had to admit, she had a pretty notorious reputation. She'd never been one to blindly follow the rules, plus there was the Haumea Incident and her imprisonment. And her family were infamous in the Space Corps. Her father had been a space marine, killed in action in one of the early Kantos encounters. Her mom had been a decorated Space Corps member, but after Eve's dad had died, her mom had started drinking. It had deteriorated until she'd gone off the rails. She'd done it quite publicly, blaming the Space Corps for her husband's death. In the process, she'd forgotten she had three young, grieving girls.

Yep, Eve was well aware that the people you cared for most either left you, or let you down. The employer you worked your ass off for treated you like shit. The only two people in the galaxy that didn't apply to were her sisters.

Eve pushed thoughts of her parents away. Instead, she scanned the starship. The *Polaris* was a good ship. A mid-size cruiser, she was designed for exploration, but well-armed as well. Eve guessed they'd be heading out beyond Neptune about now.

The plan was for the *Polaris* to take her to the edge of Eon space, where she'd take a tiny, two-person stealth ship, sneak up to the *Desteron*, then steal onboard.

Piece of cake. She rolled her eyes.

Back in her small cabin, she took a quick shower,

dressed, and then headed to the ops room. It was a small room close to the bridge that the ship's captain had made available to her.

She stepped inside, and all the screens flickered to life. A light table stood in the center of the room, and everything was filled with every scrap of intel that the Space Corps had on the Eon Empire, their warriors, the *Desteron*, and War Commander Thann-Eon.

It was more than she'd guessed. A lot of it had been classified. There was fascinating intel on the four Eon homeworld planets—Eon, Jad, Felis, and Ath. Each Eon warrior carried their homeworld in their name, along with their clan names. The war commander hailed from the planet Eon, and Thann was a clan known as a warrior clan.

Eve swiped her fingers across the light table and studied pictures of the *Desteron*. They were a few years old and taken from a great distance, but that didn't hide the warship's power.

It was fearsome. Black, sleek, and impressive. It was built for speed and stealth, but also power. It had to be packed with weapons beyond their imagination.

She touched the screen again and slid the image to the side. Another image appeared—the only known picture of War Commander Thann-Eon.

Jesus. The man packed a punch. All Eon warriors looked alike—big, broad-shouldered, muscular. They all had longish hair—not quite reaching the shoulders, but not cut short, either. Their hair usually ranged from dark brown to a tawny, golden-brown. There was no black or blond hair among the Eon. Their skin color ranged from dark-brown to light-brown, as well.

Before first contact had gone sour, both sides had done some DNA testing, and confirmed the Eon and Terrans shared an ancestor.

The war commander was wearing a pitch-black, sleeveless uniform. He was tall, built, with long legs and powerful thighs. He was exactly the kind of man you expected to stride onto a battlefield, pull a sword, and slaughter everyone. He had a strong face, one that shouted power. Eve stroked a finger over the image. He had a square jaw, a straight, almost aggressive nose, and a well-formed brow. His eyes were as dark as space, but shot through with intriguing threads of blue.

"It's you and me, War Commander." If he didn't kill her, first.

Suddenly, sirens blared.

Eve didn't stop to think. She slammed out of the ops room and sprinted onto the bridge.

Inside, the large room was a flurry of activity.

Captain Chen stood in the center of the space, barking orders at his crew.

Her heart contracted. God, she'd missed this so much. The vibration of the ship beneath her feet, her team around her, even the scent of recycled starship air.

"You shouldn't be in here," a sharp voice snapped.

Eve turned, locking gazes with the stocky, bearded XO. Sub-Captain Porter wasn't a fan of hers.

"Leave her," Captain Chen told his second-in-command. "She's seen more Kantos ships than all of us combined."

The captain looked back at his team. "Shields up."

Eve studied the screen and the Kantos ship approaching.

It looked like a bug. It had large, outstretched legs, and a bulky, segmented, central fuselage. It wasn't the biggest ship she'd seen, but it wasn't small, either. It was probably out on some intel mission.

"Sir," a female voice called out. "We're getting a distress call from the *Panama*, a cargo ship en route to Nightingale Space Station. They're under attack from a swarm of small Kantos ships."

Eve sucked in a breath, her hand curling into a fist. This was a usual Kantos tactic. They would overwhelm a ship with their small swarm ships. It had ugly memories of the Haumea Incident stabbing at her.

"Open the comms channel," the captain ordered.

"Please...help us." A harried man's voice came over the distorted comm line. "...can't hold out much...thirty-seven crew onboard...we are..."

Suddenly, a huge explosion of light flared in the distance.

Eve's shoulders sagged. The cargo ship was gone.

"Goddammit," the XO bit out.

The front legs of the larger Kantos ship in front of them started to glow orange.

"They're going to fire," Eve said.

The captain straightened. "Evasive maneuvers."

His crew raced to obey the orders, the *Polaris* veering suddenly to the right.

"The swarm ships will be on their way back." Eve knew the Kantos loved to swarm like locusts.

"Release the tridents," the captain said.

Good. Eve watched the small, triple-pronged space mines rain out the side of the ship. They'd be a dangerous minefield for the Kantos swarm.

The main Kantos ship swung around.

"They're locking weapons," someone shouted.

Eve fought the need to shout out orders and offer the captain advice. Last time she'd done that, she'd ended up in shackles.

The blast hit the *Polaris*, the shields lighting up from the impact. The ship shuddered.

"Shields holding, but depleting," another crew member called out.

"Sub-Captain Traynor?" The captain's dark gaze met hers.

Something loosened in her chest. "It's a raider-class cruiser, Captain. You're smaller and more maneuverable. You need to circle around it, spray it with laser fire. Its weak spots are on the sides. Sustained laser fire will eventually tear it open. You also need to avoid the legs."

"Fly circles around it?" a young man at a console said. "That's crazy."

Eve eyed the lead pilot. "You up for this?"

The man swallowed. "I don't think I can..."

"Sure you can, if you want us to survive this."

"Walker, do it," the captain barked.

The pilot pulled in a breath and the *Polaris* surged forward. They rounded the Kantos ship. Up close, the bronze-brown hull looked just like the carapace of an insect. One of the legs swung up, but Walker had quick reflexes.

"Fire," Eve said.

The weapons officer started firing. Laser fire hit the Kantos ship in a pretty row of orange.

"Keep going," Eve urged.

They circled the ship, firing non-stop.

Eve crossed her arms over her chest. Everything in her was still, but alive, filled with energy. She'd always known she was born to stand on the bridge of a starship.

"More," she urged. "Keep firing."

"Swarm ships incoming," a crew member yelled.

"Hold," Eve said calmly. "Trust the mines." She eyed the perspiring weapons officer. "What's your name, Lieutenant?"

"Law, ma'am. Lieutenant Miriam Law."

"You're doing fine, Law. Ignore the swarm ships and keep firing on the cruiser."

The swarm ships rushed closer, then hit the field of mines. Eve saw the explosions, like brightly colored pops of fireworks.

The lasers kept cutting into the hull of the larger Kantos ship. She watched the ship's engines fire. They were going to try and make a run for it.

"Bring us around, Walker. Fire everything you have, Law."

They swung around to face the side of the Kantos ship straight on. The laser ripped into the hull.

There was a blinding flash of light, and startled exclamations filled the bridge. She squinted until the light faded away.

On the screen, the Kantos ship broke up into pieces.

Captain Chen released a breath. "Thank you, Sub-Captain."

Eve inclined her head. She glanced at the silent crew. "Good flying, Walker. And excellent shooting, Law."

But she looked back at the screen, at the debris hanging in space and the last of the swarm ships retreating.

They'd keep coming. No matter what. It was ingrained in the Kantos to destroy.

They had to be stopped.

Eon Warriors

Edge of Eon

Touch of Eon

Heart of Eon

Kiss of Eon

Mark of Eon

Claim of Eon

Storm of Eon

Soul of Eon

King of Eon

Also Available as Audiobooks!

Want more action-packed sci-fi romance? Then check out the **Galactic Kings**.

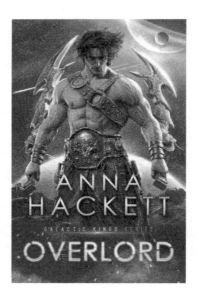

When an experimental starship test goes

horribly wrong, a test pilot from Earth is flung across the galaxy and crash lands on the planet of a powerful alien king.

Pilot Mallory West is having a really bad day. She's crashed on an alien planet, her ship is in pieces, and her best friend Poppy, the scientist monitoring the experiment, is missing. Dazed and injured, she collapses into the arms of a big, silver-eyed warrior king. But when her rescuer cuffs her to a bed and accuses her of being a spy, Mal knows she has to escape her darkly tempting captor and find her friend.

Overlord Rhain Zhalto Sarkany is in a battle to protect his planet Zhalto and his people from his evil, power-hungry father. He'll use every one of his deadly Zhalton abilities to win the fight against his father's lethal warlord and army of vicious creatures. Rhain suspects the tough, intriguing woman he pulls from a starship wreck is a trap, but when Mal escapes, he is compelled to track her down.

Fighting their overwhelming attraction, Mal and Rhain join forces to hunt down the warlord and find Poppy. But as Mal's body reacts to Zhalto's environment, it awakens dormant powers, and Rhain is the only one who can help her. As the warlord launches a brutal attack, it will take all of Mal and Rhain's combined powers to save their friends, the planet, and themselves.

Galactic Kings
Overlord

Emperor
Captain of the Guard
Conqueror
Also Available as Audiobooks!

ALSO BY ANNA HACKETT

Sentinel Security

Wolf

Hades

Striker

Steel

Excalibur

Hex

Also Available as Audiobooks!

Norcross Security

The Investigator

The Troubleshooter

The Specialist

The Bodyguard

The Hacker

The Powerbroker

The Detective

The Medic

The Protector

Also Available as Audiobooks!

Billionaire Heists

Stealing from Mr. Rich

Blackmailing Mr. Bossman

Hacking Mr. CEO

Also Available as Audiobooks!

Team 52

Mission: Her Protection

Mission: Her Rescue

Mission: Her Security

Mission: Her Defense

Mission: Her Safety

Mission: Her Freedom

Mission: Her Shield

Mission: Her Justice

Also Available as Audiobooks!

Treasure Hunter Security

Undiscovered

Uncharted

Unexplored

Unfathomed

Untraveled

Unmapped

Unidentified

Undetected

Also Available as Audiobooks!

Oronis Knights

Knightmaster

Knighthunter

Galactic Kings

Overlord

Emperor

Captain of the Guard

Conqueror

Also Available as Audiobooks!

Eon Warriors

Edge of Eon

Touch of Eon

Heart of Eon

Kiss of Eon

Mark of Eon

Claim of Eon

Storm of Eon

Soul of Eon

King of Eon

Also Available as Audiobooks!

Galactic Gladiators: House of Rone

Sentinel

Defender

Centurion

Paladin

Guard

Weapons Master

Also Available as Audiobooks!

Galactic Gladiators

Gladiator

Warrior

Hero

Protector

Champion

Barbarian

Beast

Rogue

Guardian

Cyborg

Imperator

Hunter

Also Available as Audiobooks!

Hell Squad

Marcus

Cruz

Gabe

Reed

Roth

Noah

Shaw

Holmes

Niko

Finn

Devlin

Theron

Hemi

Ash

Levi

Manu

Griff

Dom

Survivors

Tane

Also Available as Audiobooks!

The Anomaly Series

Time Thief

Mind Raider

Soul Stealer

Salvation

Anomaly Series Box Set

The Phoenix Adventures

Among Galactic Ruins

At Star's End

In the Devil's Nebula

On a Rogue Planet

Beneath a Trojan Moon

Beyond Galaxy's Edge

On a Cyborg Planet

Return to Dark Earth

On a Barbarian World

Lost in Barbarian Space

Through Uncharted Space

Crashed on an Ice World

Perma Series

Winter Fusion

A Galactic Holiday

Warriors of the Wind

Tempest

Storm & Seduction

Fury & Darkness

Standalone Titles

Savage Dragon

Hunter's Surrender

One Night with the Wolf

For more information visit www.annahackett.com

ABOUT THE AUTHOR

I'm a USA Today bestselling romance author who's passionate about ***fast-paced,*** ***emotion-filled*** contemporary romantic suspense and science fiction romance. I love writing about people overcoming unbeatable odds and achieving seemingly impossible goals. I like to believe it's possible for all of us to do the same.

I live in Australia with my own personal hero and two very busy, always-on-the-move sons.

For release dates, behind-the-scenes info, free books, and other fun stuff, sign up for the latest news here:

Website: www.annahackett.com

Made in United States
Orlando, FL
05 August 2023

35813947R00143